CAPRICE

THE NEW DIRECTIONS

Bibelots

KAY BOYLE
THE CRAZY HUNTER

RONALD FIRBANK
CAPRICE

HENRY MILLER
A DEVIL IN PARADISE

DYLAN THOMAS
EIGHT STORIES

TENNESSEE WILLIAMS
THE ROMAN SPRING OF MRS. STONE

RONALD FIRBANK

CAPRICE

A NEW DIRECTIONS

TO
STEPHEN HAMMERTON

Τίς δ'ἀγροιῶτίς τοι θέλγει νόον,
οὐκ ἐπωταμένα τὰ βράκε᾽"ἕλκην ἐπὶ τῶν σφύρων.—*Sappho.*

Manufactured in the United States of America
New Directions Books are printed on acid-free paper.
Caprice is taken from New Directions' edition of Ronald
Firbank's *Three More Novels* (1951, 1986).
First published as a New Directions Bibelot in 1993.
Published simultaneously in Canada by Penguin Books Canada
Limited.

Library of Congress Cataloging in Publication Data

Firbank, Ronald, 1886-1926.
    Caprice / Ronald Firbank.
        p.   cm.
    ISBN 0-8112-1243-2
    I. Title.
    PR6011.I7C36   1993   93-16388
    823'.912—dc20   CIP

New Directions Books are published for James Laughlin
by New Directions Publishing Corporation,
80 Eighth Avenue, New York 10011

SECOND PRINTING

I

THE clangour of bells grew insistent. In uncontrollable hilarity pealed S. Mary, contrasting clearly with the subdued carillon of S. Mark. From all sides, seldom in unison, resounded bells. S. Elizabeth and S. Sebastian, in Flower Street, seemed in loud dispute, while S. Ann " on the Hill," all hollow, cracked, consumptive, fretful, did nothing but complain. Near by S. Nicaise, half paralysed and impotent, feebly shook. Then, triumphant, in a hurricane of sound, S. Irene hushed them all.

It was Sunday again.

Up and up, and still up, the winding ways of the city the straggling townsfolk toiled.

Now and again a pilgrim perhaps would pause in the narrow lane behind the Deanery to rest.

Opening a black lacquer fan and setting the window of her bedroom wide, Miss Sarah Sinquier peered out.

The lane, very frequently, would prove interesting of an afternoon.

Across it, the Cathedral rose up before her with wizardry against the evening sky.

Miss Sinquier raised her eyes towards the twin grey spires, threw up her arms, and yawned.

From a pinnacle a devil with limbs entwined about some struggling crowned-coiffed prey grimaced.

> " For I yearn for those kisses you gave me once
>   On the steps by Bakerloo! "

Miss Sinquier crooned caressingly, craning further out.

Under the little old lime trees by the Cathedral door lounged Lady Caroline Dempsey's Catholic footman.

Miss Sinquier considered him.

In her mind's eye she saw the impression her own conversion would make in the parochial world.

" Canon Sinquier's only daughter has gone over to Rome. . . ." Or, " Canon Sinquier's daughter has taken the veil." Or, "Miss Sinquier, having suffered untold persecution at the hands of her family, has been received into the Convent of the Holy Dove."

Her eyes strayed leisurely from the powdered head and weeping shoulder-knots of Lady Caroline Dempsey's Catholic footman. The lack of movement was oppressive.

Why was not Miss Worrall in her customary collapse being borne senseless to her Gate in the Sacristan's arms? And why to-night were they not chaunting the Psalms?

Darting out her tongue, Miss Sinquier withdrew her head and resumed her book.

" Pouf! "

She shook her fan.

The room would soon be dark.

From the grey-toned walls, scriptural, a *Sasso Sassi* frowned.

" In all these fruitful years," she read, " the only time he is recorded to have smiled was when a great rat ran in and out among some statues. . . . *He* was the Ideal Hamlet. Morose of countenance, and cynical by nature, his outbursts, at times, would completely freeze the company."

Miss Sinquier passed her finger-tips lightly across her hair.

" Somehow it makes no difference," she murmured, turning towards a glass. To feign Ophelia—no matter what!

She pulled about her a lace Manilla shawl.

It was as though it were Andalusia whenever she wrapped it on.

" *Dona Rosarda!* "

" *Fernan Perez? What do you want?* "

" *Ravishing Rosarda, I need you.* "

" *I am the wife of Don José Cuchillo—the Moor.* "

" *Dona Rosarda Castilda Cuchillo, I love you.* "

" *Sh—! My husband will be back directly.* "

Stretched at ease before a pier-glass, Miss Sinquier grew enthralled.

An hour sped by.

The room was almost dark.

Don José would wish his revenge.

" *Rosarda.* "

" *Fernando?* "

" *Ah-h!* "

Miss Sinquier got up.

She must compose herself for dinner—wash off the blood.

Poor Fernan!

She glanced about her, a trifle Spanish still.

From a clothes-peg something hanging seemed to implore.

" To see me? Why, bless you. Yes! "

With an impetuous, pretty gesture she flung it upon a couch.

" How do I like America? "

" I adore it . . . You see . . . I've lost my heart here—! Tell them so—oh! especially to the men. . . . Whereabouts was I born? In Westmorland; yes. *In England, Sir!* Inquisitive? Why not at all. I was born in the sleepy peaceful town of Applethorp (three p's), in the inmost heart—right in the very middle," Miss Sinquier murmured, tucking a few wild flowers under her chin, " of the *Close.* "

" SALLY," her father said, " I could not make out where you sat at Vespers, child, to-night."

In the old-world Deanery drawing-room, coffee and liqueurs—a Sunday indulgence—had been brought in.

Miss Sinquier set down her cup.

Behind her, through the open windows, a riot of light leaves and creepers was swaying restively to and fro.

" I imagine the *Font* hid me," she answered with a little laugh.

Canon Sinquier considered with an absent air, an abundant-looking moon, then turned towards his wife.

" To-morrow, Mary," he said, " there's poor Mrs. Cushman again."

At her cylinder-desk, between two flickering candles, Mrs. Sinquier, while her coffee grew cold, was opening her heart to a friend.

" Do, Mike, keep still," she begged.

" Still? "

" Don't fidget. Don't talk."

" Or dare to breathe," her daughter added, taking up a Sunday journal and approaching nearer the light.

" ' At the Olive Theatre,' " she read, " ' Mrs. Starcross will produce a new comedy, in the coming autumn, which promises to be of the highest interest.' "

Her eyes kindled.

" O God! "

" ' At the Kehama, Yvonde Yalta will be seen shortly in a Japanese piece, with singing mandarins, geishas, and old samurai—' "

" Dear Lord! "

" ' Mr. and Mrs. Mary are said to be contemplating management again.' "

" Heavens above! "

" ' For the revival of *She Stoops to*——' "

Crescendo, across the mist-clad Close broke a sorrowful, sated voice.

" You can fasten the window, Sarah," Canon Sinquier said.

" It's Miss Biggs! "

" Who could have taught her? How? " the Canon wondered.

Mrs. Sinquier laid down her pen.

" I dread her intimate dinner! " she said.

" Is it to be intimate? "

" Isn't she always? ' Come round and see me soon, Miss Sarah, *there's* a dear, and let's be intimate!' "

" Really, Sally! "

" Sally can take off anyone."

" It's vulgar, dear, to mimic."

" Vulgar? "

" It isn't nice."

" Many people do."

" Only mountebanks."

" I'd bear a good deal to be on the stage."

Canon Sinquier closed his eyes.

" Recite, dear, something; soothe me," he said.

" Of course, if you wish it."

" Soothe me, Sally! "

" Something to obliterate the sermon? "

Miss Sinquier looked down at her feet. She had on black babouches all over little pearls with filigree butterflies that trembled above her toes.

" Since first I beheld you, Adele,
  While dancing the celinda,
  I have remained faithful to the thought of you;
  My freedom has departed from me,

5

I care no longer for all other negresses;
I have no heart left for them;—
You have such grace and cunning;—
You are like the Congo serpent."

Miss Sinquier paused.

" You need the proper movements . . . " she explained. " One ought *really* to shake one's shanks! "

" Being a day of rest, my dear, we will dispense with it."

" I love you too much, my beautiful one—
I am not able to help it.
My heart has become just like a grasshopper,—
It does nothing but leap.
I have never met any woman
Who has so beautiful a form as yours.
Your eyes flash flame;
Your body has enchained me captive.

Ah, you are like the rattlesnake
Who knows how to charm the little bird,
And who has a mouth ever ready for it
To serve it for a tomb.
I have never known any negress
Who could walk with such grace as you can,
Or who could make such beautiful gestures;
Your body is a beautiful doll.

When I cannot see you, Adele,
I feel myself ready to die;
My life becomes like a candle
Which has almost burned itself out.
I cannot then find anything in the world
Which is able to give me pleasure:

I could well go down to the river
And throw myself in so that I might cease to suffer.

Tell me if you have a man,
And I will make an ouanga charm for him;
I will make him turn into a phantom,
If you will only take me for your husband.
I will not go to see you when you are cross:
Other women are mere trash to me;
I will make you very happy
And I will give you a beautiful Madras handker-
      chief."

" Thank you, thank you, Sally."
" It is from *Ozias Midwinter*."
Mrs. Sinquier shuddered.
" Those scandalous topsies that entrap our mission-
aries! " she said.
" In Oshkosh——"
" Don't, Mike. The horrors that go on in certain
places, I'm sure no one would believe."
Miss Sinquier caressed lightly the Canon's cheek.
" Soothed? " she asked.
" . . . Fairly."
" When I think of those coloured coons," Mrs.
Sinquier went on, " at the Palace fête last year! Roam-
ing all night in the Close. . . . And when I went to
look out next day there stood an old mulattress holding
up the baker's boy in the lane."
" There, Mary! "
" Tired, dear? "
" Sunday's always a strain."
" For you, alas! it's bound to be."
" There were the Catechetical Classes to-day."
" Very soon now Sally will learn to relieve you."
Miss Sinquier threw up her eyes.
" I? " she wondered.

" Next Sunday; it's time you should begin."

" Between now and *that*," Miss Sinquier reflected, shortly afterwards, on her way upstairs, " I shall almost certainly be in town."

" O London—City of Love! " she warbled softly as she locked her door.

In the gazebo at the extremity of the garden, by the new parterre, Miss Sinquier, in a morning wrapper, was waiting for the post.

Through the trellis chinks, semi-circular, showed the Close, with its plentiful, seasoned timber and sedate, tall houses, a stimulating sequence, architecturally, of whitewash, stone and brick.

Miss Sinquier stirred impatiently.

Wretch!—to deliver at the Palace before the Deanery, when the Deanery was as near!

" Shower down over there, O Lord, ten thousand fearsome bills," extemporaneously she prayed, " and spare them not at all. Amen."

Hierarchic hands shot upwards.

Dull skies.

She waited.

Through the Palace gates, at length, the fellow lurched, sorting as he came.

" Dolt! "

Her eyes devoured his bag.

Coiled round and round like some sleek snake her future slumbered in it.

Husband; lovers . . . little lives, perhaps—yet to be . . . besides voyages, bouquets, diamonds, chocolates, duels, casinos! . . .

She shivered.

" Anything for me, Hodge, to-day," she inquired, " by chance? "

" A fine morning, miss."

" Unusually."

It had come . . .

That large mauve envelope, with the wild hand-writing and the haunting scent was from *her*.

As she whisked away her heart throbbed fast. Through the light spring foliage she could see her father, with folded hands, pacing meditatively to and fro before the front of the house.

" Humbug! " she murmured, darting down a gravel path towards the tradesmen's door.

Regaining her room, she promptly undid the seal.

" Panvale Priory, Shaftesbury Avenue,
" London, W.

" Mrs. Albert Bromley presents her compliments to Miss S. Sinquier and will be pleased to offer her her experience and advice on Thursday morning next at the hour Miss Sinquier names.

" *P.S.* Mrs. Bromley already feels a parent's sympathetic interest in Miss Sinquier. Is she dark or fair?. . . Does she shape for Lady Macbeth or is she a Lady Teazle? "

" Both! " Miss Sinquier gurgled, turning a deft somersault before the glass.

To keep the appointment, without being rushed, she would be obliged to set out, essentially baggage-less, to-night—a few requisites merely, looped together and concealed beneath her dress, would be the utmost she could manage.

" A lump here and a lump there! " she breathed, " and I can unburden myself in the train."

" Okh! "

She peeped within her purse.

. . . And there was Godmother's chain that she would sell!

It should bring grist; perhaps close on a thousand pounds. Misericordia: to be compelled to part with it!

Opening a levant-covered box, she drew out a long flat tray.

Adorable pearls!

How clearly now they brought her Godmother to mind . . . a little old body . . . with improbable cherry-cheeks and excrescent upper lip, with always the miniatures of her three deceased husbands clinging about one arm. . . . " Aren't they pleasant? " she would say proudly every now and then. . . . What talks they had had; and sometimes of an evening through the mauve moonlight they would strut together.

Ah! She had been almost ugly then; clumsy, gawky, *gauche* . . .

Now that she was leaving Applethorp, for ever perhaps, how dormant impressions revived!

The Saunders' Fifeshire bull. one New Year's night, ravaging the Close, driven frantic by the pealings of the bells. The time poor Dixon got drowned—at a Flower Show, a curate's eyes—a German governess's walk—a mould of calves'-foot jelly she had let fall in the Cathedral once, on her way somewhere——

She replaced ruefully her pearls.

What else?

Her artist fingers hovered.

Mere bridesmaid's rubbish; such frightful frippery.

She turned her thoughts to the room.

Over the bed, an antique bush-knife of barbaric shape, supposed to have been *Abraham's*, was quite a collector's piece.

It might be offered to some museum perhaps. The Nation ought to have it . . .

She sighed shortly.

And downstairs in the butler's room there were possessions of hers, besides. What of those Apostle spoons, and the two-pronged forks, and the chased tureen?

Leonard frequently had said it took the best part of a day to polish her plate alone.

And to go away and leave it all!

" O God, help me, Dear," she prayed. " This little once, O Lord! For Thou knowest my rights . . ."

She waited.

Why did not an angel with a basket of silver appear?

" Oh, well . . ."

Gripper, no doubt, would suspect something odd if she asked for her things " to play with " for an hour. . . .

A more satisfactory scheme would be to swoop into the pantry, on her way to the station, and to take them away for herself.

She had only to say, " Make haste with them crevets," for Gripper to go off in a huff, and Leonard, should he be there, would be almost sure to follow.

Men were so touchy.

Hush!

Her mother's voice came drifting from below.

" Kate! Kate! Kate! Kate! "

She listened.

" Have the chintz curtains in the white room folded," she could hear her say, " and remember what I said about the carpet . . ."

Dear soul!

Miss Sinquier sniffed.

Was it a tear?

Dear soul! Dear souls! . . .

" Never mind," she murmured, " they shall have *sofas* in their box on the night of my debut . . ."

She consoled herself with the thought.

I V

"MAKE haste now with them crevets!"

"For shame, miss. I shall go straight to the Dean!"

"Cr-r-r-evets!" Miss Sinquier called.

Clad in full black, with a dark felt *chapeau de résistance* and a long Lancastrian shawl, she felt herself no mean match for any man.

"C-r-r-r," she growled, throwing back her shawl.

After all, were not the things her own?

She laughed gaily.

"If dear Mrs. Bromley could see me," she beamed, tucking dexterously away an apostolic spoon.

> "' St. Matthew—St. Mark—St. Luke—St. John—
> *These* sprang into bed with their breeches on.'"

At a friendly frolic once a Candidate for Orders had waltzed her about to that.

She recalled Fräulein's erudite query still:

"Pray, why did they not take off all like the others?"

And the young man's significant reasons and elaborate suppositions, and Fräulein's creamy tone as she said she *quite* understood.

Miss Sinquier turned a key.

S-s-s-st!

"Butter fingers."

In a moment she must run.

Terrible to forgo her great tureen . . .

She poked it. What magnitude to be sure!

Impossible to tow it along.

Under the circumstances, why not take something less cumbersome instead?

13

There were the Caroline sauce-boats, or the best Anne teapot, hardly if ever in use.

Her ideas raced on.

And who could resist those gorgeous grapes, for the train?

Together with their dish . . .

" Tudor, ' Harry '! " she breathed.

From the corridor came a hum of voices.

Flinging her wrap about her, Miss Sinquier slipped quietly out by way of a small room, where the Canon preserved his lawn.

Outside, the moon was already up—a full moon, high and white, a wisp of cloud stretched across it like a blindfold face.

Oh Fame, dear!

She put up her face.

Across the garden the Cathedral loomed out of a mist as white as milk.

The damp, she reasoned, alone would justify her flight!

She shivered.

How sombre it looked in the lane.

There were roughs there frequently too.

" Villains . . ."

She felt fearfully her pearls.

After all, the initial step in any career was usually reckoned the worst.

Some day, at the King's, or the Canary, or the Olive, in the warmth of a stage dressing-room, she would be amused, perhaps, and say:

" I left my father's roof, sir, one sweet spring night —without so much as a word! "

V

RAINDROPS were falling although the sky was visibly brightening as Miss Sinquier, tired, and a little uncertain, passed through the main exit of Euston terminus.

She wavered a moment upon the curb.

On a hoarding, as if to welcome her, a dramatic poster of Fan Fisher unexpectedly warmed her heart; it was almost like being met . . .

There stood Fan, at concert pitch, as Masha Olga-ruski in *The Spy*.

Miss Sinquier tingled.

A thing like that was enough to give one wings for a week.

She set off briskly, already largely braced.

Before meeting Mrs. Bromley on the morrow much would have to be done.

There was the difficulty of lodgment to consider.

Whenever she had been in the metropolis before she had stayed at *Millars* in Eric Street, overlooking Percy Place; because Mr. Millar had formerly been employed at the Deanery, and had, moreover, married their cook. . . .

But before going anywhere she must acquire a trunk.

Even Church dignitaries had been known to be refused accommodation on arriving at a strange hotel with nothing but themselves.

She threw a glance upwards towards a clock.

It was early yet!

All the wonderful day stretched before her, and in the evening she would take a ticket perhaps for some light vaudeville or new revue.

She studied the pleasure announcements on the motor-buses as they swayed along.

Stella Starcross—The Lady from the Sea—This evening, Betty Buttermilk and Co.—Rose Tournesol —Mr. and Mrs. Mary's Season: The Carmelite—The Shop Boy—Clemenza di Tito. To-night!

Miss Sinquier blinked.

Meanwhile the family teapot was becoming a bore.

Until the shops should open up it might be well to take a taxi and rest in the Park for an hour.

The weather was clearing fast; the day showed signs of heat.

She hailed a passing cab.

" Hyde Park," she murmured, climbing slowly in.

She thrilled.

Upon the floor and over the cushions of the cab were sprinkled fresh confetti—turquoise, pink and violet, gold and green.

She took up some.

As a mascot, she reflected, it would be equivalent to a cinqfoil of clover, or a tuft of edelweiss, or a twist of hangman's rope.

VI

FROM the big hotel in the vicinity of the Marble Arch, to the consulting rooms in Shaftesbury Avenue of Mrs. Albert Bromley, it appeared, on inquiry, that the distance might easily be accomplished in less than forty minutes.

Miss Sinquier, nevertheless, decided to allow herself more.

Garmented charmingly in a cornflower-blue frock with a black gauze turban trimmed with a forest of tinted leaves, she lingered, uplifted by her appearance, before the glass.

The sober turban, no doubt, would suggest to Mrs. Bromley Macbeth—the forest-scene, and the blue, she murmured, " might be anything."

It occurred to her as she left her room that Mr. Bromley might quite conceivably be there to assist his wife.

" Odious if he is," she decided, passing gaily out into the street.

It was just the morning for a walk. A pale silvery light spread over Oxford Street, while above the shop fronts the sun flashed down upon a sea of brass-tipped masts, from whence trade flags trembled in a vagrant breeze. Rejoicing in her independence, and in the exhilarating brightness of the day, Miss Sinquier sailed along. The ordeal of a first meeting with a distinguished dramatic expert diminished at every step. She could conjecture with assurance, almost, upon their ultimate mutual understanding. But before expressing any opinion, Mrs. Bromley, no doubt, would require to test her voice; perhaps, also, expect her to dance and declaim.

Miss Sinquier thrust out her lips.

" Not before Albert! Or at any rate not yet . . ."
she muttered.

She wondered what she knew.

There was the thing from *Rizzio*. The Mistress of
the Robes' lament upon her vanished youth, on dis-
covering a mirror unexpectedly, one morning, at
Holyrood, outside Queen Mary's door.

Diamond, Lady Drummond, bearing the Queen a
cap, raps, smiles, listens . . . smiles, raps again, puts out
her leg and rustles . . . giggles, ventures to drop a ring,
effusive facial play and sundry tentative noises, when,
catching sight of her reflection, she starts back with:

" O obnoxious old age! O hideous horror! O
youthful years all gone! O childhood spent! Decrepi-
tude at hand . . . Infirmities drawing near. . . ."

Interrupted by Mary's hearty laugh.

" Yes," Miss Sinquier decided, crossing into Regent
Street, " should Mrs. Bromley bid me declaim, I'll do
Diamond."

Her eyes brightened.

How prettily the street swerved.

As a rule, great thoroughfares were free from tricks.
She sauntered.

" A picture-palace."

And just beyond were the playhouses themselves.
Theatreland!

Shaftesbury Avenue with its slightly foreign aspect
stretched before her.

With a springing foot she turned up it.

Oh, those fragile glass façades with the players'
names suspended!

There was the new Merrymount Theatre with its
roguish Amorini supporting torches and smiling down
over gay flower-boxes on to the passers-by.

And beyond, where the burgeoning trees began,
must be Panvale Priory itself.

Miss Sinquier surveyed it.

It looked to be public offices. . . .

On the mat, dressed in a violet riband, with its paw in the air, lay a great sly, black, joyous cat.

" Toms! "

She scratched it.

Could it be Mrs. Bromley's?

In the threshold, here and there, were small brass plates, that brought to mind somehow memorial tablets to departed virtue at home.

Miss Sinquier studied the inscriptions.

Ah, there showed hers!

" M-m-m! " she murmured, commencing to climb.

Under the skylight a caged bird was singing shrilly.

As much to listen as to brush something to her cheeks, Miss Sinquier paused.

If a microscopic mirror could be relied upon she had seldom looked so well.

Scrambling up the remaining stairs with alacrity, she knocked.

A maid with her head wreathed in curl-papers answered the door, surveying the visitor first through a muslin blind.

Miss Sinquier pulled out a card.

" Is Mrs. Bromley in? " she asked.

The woman gazed at her feet.

" Mrs. Bromley's gone! " she replied.

" I suppose she won't be long? "

" She's in Elysium."

" At the———? "

" Poor Mrs. Bromley's dead."

" Mrs. Bromley *dead* . . .? "

" Poor Mrs. Bromley died last night."

Miss Sinquier staggered.

" Impossible! "

" Perhaps you'd care to come in and sit down? "

Miss Sinquier hesitated.

" No, no, not if . . . *is?* Oh! " she stammered.

" She was taken quite of a sudden."

" One can hardly yet believe it? "

" She'll be a loss to her world, alas, poor Betty Bromley will!"

Miss Sinquier swallowed.

" I should like to attend the funeral," she said.

" There's no funeral."

" No funeral? "

" No invitations, that is."

Miss Sinquier turned away.

The very ground under her seemed to slide . . .

Mrs. Bromley dead!

Why, the ink of her friendly note seemed scarcely dry!

On the pavement once more she halted to collect herself.

Who was there left at all?

At Croydon there was a conservatoire, of course—

She felt a little guilty at the rapidity of the idea.

Wool-gathering, she breasted the traffic in St. Martin's Lane.

She would turn over the situation presently more easily in the Park.

Instinctively, she stopped to examine a portrait of Yvonde Yalta in the open vestibule of the Dream.

She devoured it: Really . . . ? Really? She resembled more some Girton guy than a great coquette.

All down the street indeed, at the theatre doors, were studies of artists, scenes from current plays.

By the time she found herself back in Piccadilly Circus again Miss Sinquier was nearly fainting from inanition.

She peered around.

In Regent Street, she reflected, almost certainly, there must be some nice tea-shop, some cool creamery . . .

How did this do?

" The Café Royal! "

Miss Sinquier fluttered in.

By the door, the tables all proved to be taken.

Such a noise!

Everyone seemed to be chattering, smoking, lunching, casting dice, or playing dominoes.

She advanced slowly through a veil of opal mist, feeling her way from side to side with her parasol.

It was like penetrating deeper and deeper into a bath.

She put out her hand in a swimming, groping gesture, twirling as she did so, accidentally, an old gentleman's moustache.

Thank heaven! There, by that pillar, was a vacant place.

She sank down on to the edge of a crowded couch, as in a dream.

The tall mirrors that graced the walls told her she was tired.

" Bring me some China tea," she murmured to a passing waiter, " and a bun with currants in it."

She leaned back.

The realisation of her absolute loneliness overcame her suddenly.

Poor Mrs. Bromley, poor kindly little soul!

The tears sprang to her eyes.

It would have been a relief to have blotted her face against some neighbouring blouse or waistcoat and to have had a hearty cry.

" Excuse me, may I ask you to be so good——"

Just before her on the table was a stand for matches.

With a mournful glance she slid the apparatus from her in the direction of an adolescent of a sympathetic, somewhat sentimental, appearance, who, despite emphatic whiskers, had the air of a wildly pretty girl.

To have cherished such a one as a brother! Miss Sinquier reflected, as the waiter brought her tea.

While consuming it she studied the young man's chiselled profile from the corners of her eyes.

Supporting his chin upon the crook of a cane, he was listening, as if enthralled, to a large florid man, who, the centre of a small rapt group, was relating in a high-pitched, musical voice, how " Poor dear Chaliapin one day had asked for Kvass and was given Bass. And that reminds me," the speaker said, giving the table an impressive thump, " of the time when Anna Held—let go."

Miss Sinquier glowed.

Here were stage folk, artists, singers . . . that white thin girl in the shaggy hat opposite was without doubt a temperament akin.

She felt drawn to speak.

" Can you tell me how I should go to Croydon? " she asked.

The words came slowly, sadly almost . . .

" To Croydon? "

" You can't go to Croydon."

" Why not? "

The young man of the whiskers looked amused.

" When we all go to Spain to visit Velasquez——"

" Goya——! "

" Velasquez! "

" Goya! Goya! Goya! "

" . . . We'll set you on your way."

" Goose! "

" One goes to Croydon best by Underground," the pale-looking girl remarked.

Miss Sinquier winced.

" Underground! "

Her lip quivered.

" Is there anything the matter? "

" Only—— "

Folding her arms upon the table she sank despairingly forward and burst into tears.

"Poor Mrs. Bromley!" she sobbed.

"In the name of *Fortune* . . ." The pale young woman wondered.

"What has Serephine said? What has Mrs. Six-smith done?"

"Monstrous tease!"

The stout man wagged a finger.

"Wicked!" he commented.

The lady addressed kindled.

"I merely advised her to go Underground. By tube."

"O God." Miss Sinquier shook.

"It's hysteria. Poor thing, you can see she's over-wrought."

"Give her a *fine; un bon petit cognac.*"

"Waiter!"

"Garçon."

"Never mind, Precious," the fat man crooned. "You shall ride in a comfy taxi-cab with me."

"No; indeed she shan't," Mrs. Sixsmith snapped. "You may rely on me, Ernest, for that!"

Rejecting the proffered spirits with a gesture, Miss Sinquier controlled her grief.

"It's not *often* I'm so silly," she said.

"There, there!"

"Excuse this exhibition. . . ."

Mrs. Sixsmith squeezed her hand.

"My poor child," she said, "I fear you've had a shock."

"It's over now."

"I'm so glad."

"You've been very good."

"Not at all. You interest me."

"Why?"

"Why? Why? . . . I'm sure I can't say *why!* But directly I saw you . . ."

"It's simply wonderful."

" You marched in here for all the world like some great coquette."

" You mean the Father Christmas at the door? "

" Tell me what had happened."

In a few words Miss Sinquier recounted her tale.

" My dear," Mrs. Sixsmith said, " I shouldn't think of it again. I expect this Mrs. Bromley was nothing but an old procuress."

" A procuress? "

" A stage procuress."

" How dreadful it sounds."

" Have you no artistic connections in town *at all?*"

" Not really . . ."

" Then here, close at hand . . . sitting with you and me," she informally presented, " is Mr. Ernest Stubbs, whose wild wanderings in the Gog-magog hills in sight of Cambridge, orchestrally described, recently thrilled us all. Next to him—tuning his locks and twisting his cane—you'll notice Mr. Harold Weathercock, an exponent of calf-love parts at the Dream. And, beyond, blackening her nose with a cigarette, sprawls the most resigned of women—Miss Whipsina Peters, a daughter of the famous flagellist —and a coryphée herself."

Miss Peters nodded listlessly.

" Toodle-doo," she murmured.

" As a coryphée, I suppose her diamonds are a sight? "

" A sight!" Mrs. Sixsmith closed her eyes. "They're all laid up in lavender, I fear."

" In lavender? "

" Pledged."

" Oh, poor soul!"

" Just now you spoke of a necklace of your own . . . a pearl rope, or something, that you wish to sell."

" Unhappily I'm obliged."

" I've a notion I might be of service in the matter."

" How? "

" Through an old banker-friend of mine—Sir Oliver Dawtry. Down Hatton Garden way and throughout the City he has enormous interests. And I should say *he* could place your pearls—if anyone could! "

" Do you think he'd be bothered? "

" That I'll undertake. "

" Does he live in town? "

" In a sense: he has a large house in the Poultry. "

" Of course I should be willing to show him my pearls. "

" Sir Oliver is offering me a little dinner to-night. And I should be happy for you to join us. "

" Oh? . . . I think I scarcely dare! "

" Rubbish! One must be bolder than that if one means to get on! "

" Tell me where you dine. "

" At Angrezini's. It's a little restaurant . . . with a nigger band. And we sing between the courses. "

" Will Mr. Sixsmith be there? "

" My dear, Mr. Sixsmith and I don't live together any more. "

" Forgive me. "

" That's all right . . . "

Miss Sinquier's eyes grew dim.

" Used he to act? " she asked.

" *Act!* "

" I seem to have heard of him. "

Mrs. Sixsmith looked away.

"Are you coming, Serephine?" her neighbour asked.

" Are you all off? "

The florid man nodded impressively.

" Yes . . . we're going now . . ." he said.

" What are Whipsina's plans? "

Miss Peters leaned closely forward over several pairs of knees.

"I shall stay where I am," she murmured, "and perhaps take a nap. There's sure to be a tremendous exodus directly."

Miss Sinquier rose. "I've some shopping," she said, "to do."

"Until this evening, then."

"At what o'clock?"

"At eight."

"On arrival, am I to ask for you?"

"Better ask for Sir Oliver—one never knows . . . And I might perhaps happen to be late."

"But you won't be? You mustn't . . ."

"I will explain whatever's needful by telephone to Sir Oliver now. And during dinner," Mrs. Sixsmith bubbled, "while the old gentleman picks a quail, we will see what we can do!"

"How can I express my thanks . . .?"

"The question of commission," Mrs. Sixsmith murmured with a slight smile, "we will discuss more fully later on."

VII

SUBJECTIVE. On a rack in the loom. Powerless one-self to grasp the design. Operated on by others. At the mercy of chance fingers, unskilled fingers, tender fingers; nails of all sorts. Unable to progress alone. Finding fulfilment through friction and because of friction. Stung into sentiency gradually, bit by bit—a toe at a time.

After all there was a *zest* in it; and who should blame the raw material should an accident occur by the way . . .

Careless of an intriguing world about her, Miss Sinquier left her hotel, just so as to arrive at An-grezini's last.

"For Thou knowest well my safety is in *Thee*," she murmured to herself mazily as her taxi skirted the Park.

Having disposed of her Anne teapot for close on seventy pounds, she was looking more radiant than ever in a frail Byzantine tunic that had cost her fifty guineas.

"Thy Sally's safety," she repeated, absently scanning the Park.

Through the shadowy palings it slipped away, abundantly dotted with lovers. Some were plighting themselves on little chairs, others preferred the green ground: and beyond them, behind the whispering trees, the sky gleamed pale and luminous as church glass.

Glory to have a lover too, she reflected, and to stroll leisurely-united through the evening streets, between an avenue of sparkling lamps . . .

Her thoughts turned back to the young man in the Café Royal.

"Of all the bonny loves!" she breathed, as her taxi stopped.

"Angrezini!"

A sturdy negro helped her out.

"For Thou knowest very well——" her lips moved faintly.

The swinging doors whirled her in.

She found herself directly in a small bemirrored room with a hatch on one side of it, in which an old woman in a voluminous cap was serenely knitting.

Behind her dangled furs and wraps that scintillated or made pools of heavy shade as they caught or missed the light.

Relinquishing her own strip of tulle, Miss Sinquier turned about her.

Through a glass door she could make out Mrs. Sixsmith herself, seated in a cosy red-walled sitting-room beyond.

She was looking staid as a porcelain goddess in a garment of trailing white with a minute griffin-eared dog peeping out its sheeny paws and head wakefully from beneath her train.

At sight of her guest Mrs. Sixsmith smiled and rose.

"Sir Oliver hasn't yet come!" she said, imprinting on Miss Sinquier's youthful cheek a salute of *hospitality*.

"He hasn't? And I made sure I should be last."

Mrs. Sixsmith consulted the time.

"From the Bank to the Poultry, and from the Poultry on . . . just consider," she calculated, subsiding leisurely with Miss Sinquier upon a spindle-legged settee.

"You telephoned?"

"I told him all your story."

"Well?"

" He has promised me to do his utmost."

" He will? "

" You should have heard us. This Mrs. Bromley, he pretends . . . Oh, well . . . one must not be too harsh on the dead."

" Poor little woman."

" Let me admire your frock."

" You like it? "

" I never saw anything so waggish."

" No, no, *please*——! "

" Tell me where they are! "

" What? "

" I'm looking for your pearls."

" They're in my hair."

" Show me."

" I'll miss them terribly."

" Incline! "

" How? "

" More."

" I can't! "

" They're very nice. But bear in mind one thing ——"

" Yes? "

Mrs. Sixsmith slipped an encircling arm about Miss Sinquier's waist.

" Always remember," she said, " to a City man, twelve hundred sounds less than a thousand. Just as a year, to you and me, sounds more than eighteen months! "

" I'll not forget."

" Here is Sir Oliver now."

Through the swing doors an elderly man with a ruddy, rather apoplectic face, and close-set opaque eyes, precipitantly advanced.

" Ladies! "

" ' Ladies ' indeed, Sir Oliver."

" As if——"

" Monster."

" Excuse me, Serephine."

" Your pardon rests with Miss Sinquier," Mrs. Sixsmith said with melodious inflections as she showed the way towards the restaurant. " Address your petitions to her."

In the crescent-shaped, cedar-walled, cedar-beamed room, a table at a confidential angle had been reserved.

" There's a big gathering here to-night," Sir Oliver observed, glancing round him, a " board-room " mask clinging to him still.

Miss Sinquier looked intellectual.

" I find it hot! " she said.

" You do."

" I find London really very hot. . . . It's after the north, I suppose. In the north it's always much cooler."

" Are you from the north? "

" Yes, indeed she is," Mrs. Sixsmith chimed in. " And so am *I*," she said. " Two north-country girls!" she added gaily.

Sir Oliver spread sentimentally his feet.

" The swans at Blenheim; the peacocks at Warwick! " he sighed.

" What do you mean, Sir Oliver? "

" Intimate souvenirs . . ."

" I should say so. . . . Swans and peacocks! I wonder you're prepared to admit it."

" Admit it? "

" Outside of *Confessions*, Sir Oliver."

Miss Sinquier raised a hurried hand to her glass.

" No, no, no, no, no, no wine! " she exclaimed. " Something milky . . ."

" Fiddlesticks! Our first little dinner."

" Oh, Sir Oliver!"

" And not, I trust, our last! "

" I enjoy it so much—going out."

Mrs. Sixsmith slapped her little dog smartly upon the eyes with her fan.

" Couch-toi," she admonished.

" What can fret her? "

" She fancies she sees Paul."

" Worthless fellow! " Sir Oliver snapped.

" I was his rib, Sir Oliver."

" Forget it."

" I can't forget it."

" J-j-j——"

" Only this afternoon I ran right into him—it was just outside the Café Royal . . ."

" Scamp."

" He looked superb. Oh, so smart; spats, speckled trousers, the rest all deep indigo. Rather Russian."

" Who? "

" My actor-husband, Paul. There. One has only to speak his name for Juno to jerk her tail."

" With whom is he at present? "

" With Sydney Iphis."

" We went last night to see Mrs. Starcross," Sir Oliver said.

" She's no draw."

" I long to see her," Miss Sinquier breathed.

" I understand, my dear young lady, you've an itch for the footlights yourself."

Miss Sinquier began eating crumbs at random.

" God knows! " she declared.

" C'est une âme d'élite, Sir Oliver."

" You've no experience at all? "

" None."

Sir Oliver refused a dish.

" We old ones . . ." he lamented. " Once upon a time, I was in closer touch with the stage."

" Even so, Sir Oliver, you still retain your footing."

" Footing, f-f-f——; among the whole demned lot, who persists still but, perhaps, the Marys? "

" Take the Marys. A word to them; just think what a boon! "

" Nothing so easy."

Miss Sinquier clasped her hands.

" One has heard of them often, of course."

" Mr. and Mrs. Mary have won repute throughout the realm," Mrs. Sixsmith impressively said, wondering (as middlewoman) what commission she should ask.

" Mrs. Mary, I dare say, is no longer what she was!"

" Mrs. Mary, *aujourd'hui*, is a trifle, perhaps, full-blown, but she's most magnetic still. And a warmer, quicker heart never beat in any breast."

" In her heyday, Sir Oliver—but you wouldn't have seen her, of course."

The baronet's eyes grew extinct.

" In my younger days," he said, " she was comeliness itself . . . full of fun. I well recall her as the ' wife ' in *Macbeth;* I assure you she was positively roguish."

" Being fairly on now in years," Miss Sinquier reflected, " she naturally wouldn't fill very juvenile parts—which would be a blessing."

" She too often does."

" She used to make Paul ill——" Mrs. Sixsmith began, but stopped discreetly. " Oh, listen," she murmured, glancing up towards the nigger band and insouciantly commencing to hum.

" What is it . . .? "

" It's the *Belle of Benares*—

" ' My other females all yellow, fair or black,
    To thy charms shall prostrate fall,
    As every kind of elephant does
    To the white elephant Buitenack.
    And thou alone shall have from me,
    Jimminy, Gomminy, whee, whee, whee,
    The Gomminy, Jimminy, whee.' "

" Serephine, you're eating nothing at all."

" I shall wait for the *pâtisserie*, Sir Oliver."

" Disgraceful."

" Father Francis forbids me meat; it's a little novena he makes me do.

> " ' The great Jaw-waw that rules our land,
>   And pearly Indian sea,
>   Has not such *ab-solute* command
>   As thou hast over me,
>   With a Jimminy, Gomminy, Gomminy,
>   Jimminy, Jimminy, Gomminy, whee.' "

" Apropos of pearls ·. . ." Sir Oliver addressed Miss Sinquier, " I look forward to the privilege before long of inspecting your own."

" They're on her head, Sir Oliver! "

Sir Oliver started as a plate was passed unexpectedly over him from behind.

" Before approaching some City firm, it's possible Lady Dawtry might welcome an opportunity of acquiring this poor child's jewels for herself," Mrs. Sixsmith said.

" Lady Dawtry! "

" Why not? "

" Lady Dawtry seldom wears ornaments; often I wish she would."

" I wonder you don't *insist*."

Sir Oliver fetched a sigh.

" Many's the time," he said, " I've asked her to be a little more spectacular—but she won't."

" How women do vary! " Mrs. Sixsmith covertly smiled.

" To be sure."

" My poor old friend . . .? "

Sir Oliver turned away.

" I notice Miss Peters here to-night," he said.

33

" Whipsina? "

" With two young men."

" *Un trio n'excite pas de soupçons*, they say."

" They do . . ."

" Have you a programme for presently, Sir Oliver?"

" I've a box at the Kehama."

Miss Sinquier looked tragic.

" It'll have begun! " she said.

" At a variety, the later the better as a rule."

" I never like to miss *any* part."

" My dear, you'll miss very little; besides it's too close to linger over dinner long."

" Toc, toc; I don't find it so," Sir Oliver demurred.

Mrs. Sixsmith plied her fan.

" I feel very much like sitting, *à la* Chaste Suzanne, in the nearest ice-pail! " she declared.

VIII

MARY LODGE, or Maryland, as it was more familiarly known, stood quite at the end of Gardingore Gate, facing the Park.

Half-way down the row, on the Knightsbridge side, you caught a glimpse of it set well back in its strip of garden with a curtain of rustling aspen-trees before the door.

Erected towards the close of the eighteenth century as a retreat for a fallen minister, it had, on his demise, become the residence of a minor member of the reigning Royal House, from whose executors, it had, in due course, passed into the hands of the first histrionic couple in the land.

A gravel sweep leading between a pair of grotesquely attenuated sphinxes conducted, via a fountain, to the plain, sober façade in the Grecian style.

Moving demurely up this approach some few minutes prior to the hour telegraphically specified by the mistress of the house, Miss Sinquier, clad in a light summer dress, with a bow like a great gold butterfly under her chin, pulled the bell of Mary Lodge.

Some day Others would be standing at her own front gate, their hearts a-hammer . . .

A trim manservant answered the door.

" Is Mrs. Mary . . .? "

" Please to come this way."

Miss Sinquier followed him in.

The entrance hall bare but for a porphyry sarcophagus containing visiting cards, and a few stiff chairs, clung obviously to royal tradition still.

To right and left of the broad stairway two colossal battle-pictures, by Uccello, were narrowly divided by a pedestalled recess in which a frowning bust of Mrs. Mary as Medusa was enshrined.

Miss Sinquier, following closely, was shown into a compartment whose windows faced the Park.

" Mrs. Mary has not yet risen from lunch," the man said as he went away. " But she won't be many minutes."

Selecting herself a chair with a back suited to the occasion, Miss Sinquier prepared to wait.

It was an irregularly planned, rather lofty room, connected by a wide arch with other rooms beyond. From the painted boiseries hung glowing Eastern carpets, on which warriors astride fleet-legged fantastic horses were seen to pursue wild animals, that fled helter-skelter through transparent thickets of may. A number of fragile French chairs formed a broken ring about a Louis XVI bed—all fretted, massive pillars of twisted, gilded wood—converted now to be a seat. Persian and Pesaro pottery conserving " eternal " grasses, fans of feathers, strange sea-shells, bits of Blue-John, blocks of malachite, morsels of coral, images of jade littered the *guéridons* and *étagères*. A portrait of Mrs. Mary, by Watts, was suspended above the chimney-place, from whence came the momentous ticking of a clock.

" The old girl's lair, no doubt! " Miss Sinquier reflected, lifting her eyes towards a carved mythological ceiling describing the Zodiac and the Milky Way.

Tongue protruding, face upturned, it was something to mortify her for ever that Mrs. Mary, entering quietly, should so get her unawares.

" Look on your left."

" Oh? "

" And you'll see it; in trine of Mars. The Seventh House. The House of *Marriage*. The House of Happiness."

" Oh! Mrs. Mary! "

" You're fond of astrology? "

" I know very little about the heavenly bodies."

" Ah! *Don't* be too impatient there."

Miss Sinquier stared.

Mrs. Mary was large and robust, with commanding features and an upright carriage. She had a Redfern gown of " navy " blue stuff infinitely laced. One white long hand, curved and jewelled, clung as if paralysed above her breast.

Seating herself majestically, with a glance of invitation to Miss Sinquier to do the same, the eminent actress appraised her visitor slowly with a cold, dry eye.

" And so you're his ' little mouse '! . . ."

" Whose? "

" Sir Oliver's ' second Siddons.' "

" Indeed—— "

" Well, and what is your forte? "

" My forte, Mrs. Mary? "

" Comedy? Tragedy? "

" Either. Both come easy."

" You've no bent? "

" So long as the part is good."

" ' Sarah '! Are you of Jewish stock?—Sarahs sometimes are! "

" Oh dear no."

" Tell me something of the home circle. Have you brothers, sisters? "

" Neither."

" Is your heart free? "

" Quite."

" The Boards, I believe, are new to you? "

" Absolutely."

" Kindly stand."

" I'm five full feet."

" Say, ' Abyssinia.' "

" Abyssinia! "

" As I guessed . . ."

" I was never there."

" Now say ' Joan.' "

" Joan! "

" You're Comedy, my dear. Distinctly! And now sit down."

Miss Sinquier gasped.

" You know with us it's Repertoire, I suppose? "

" Of course."

" In parts such as one would cast Jane Jacks you should score."

" Is she giving up? "

" Unfortunately she's obliged. She's just had another babelet, poor dear."

" What were her parts? "

" In *Bashful Miss Bardine* the governess was one of them."

" Oh! "

" And in *Lara* she was the orphan. That part should suit you well," Mrs. Mary murmured, rising and taking from a cabinet a bundle of printed sheets.

" Is it rags? "

" Rags? "

" May she . . . is she allowed Evening dress? "

" Never mind about her dress. Let me hear how you'd deliver her lines," Mrs. Mary tartly said, placing in Miss Sinquier's hands a brochure of the play.

" I should like to know my cue."

" A twitter of birds is all. You are now in Lord and Lady Lara's garden—near Nice. Begin."

" *How full the hedges are of roses!* "

" Speak up."

" *How full the hedges are of roses! What perfume to be sure.*"

" And don't do that."

" The directions are: ' *she stoops.*' "

" Continue! "

" What's next? "

" A start."

" *Oh! Sir Harry!* "

" Proceed."

Miss Sinquier lodged a complaint.

" How can I when I don't know the plot? "

" What does it matter—the plot? "

" Besides, I feel up to something stronger."

Mrs. Mary caressed the backs of her books.

" Then take the slave in *Arsinoe* and I'll read out the queen."

" These little legs, Mrs. Mary, would look queerly in tights."

" Think less of your costume, dear, do; and learn to do what you're told. Begin! "

" Arsinoe opens."

" Arsi——? So she does. You should understand we're in Egypt, in the halls of Ptolemy Philadelphus, on the banks of the River Nile. I will begin.

Cease . . . Cease your song. Arisba! Lotos! THANKS.
And for thy pains accept this ivory pin . . .
Shall it be said in many-gated Thebes
That Arsinoe's mean?
The desert wind . . .
Hark to't!
Methinks 'twill blow all night;.
Lashing the lebbek trees anent Great Cheops' Pyre;
Tracing sombre shadows o'er its stony walls.
Within the wombats wail
Tearing the scarabs from Prince Kamphé's tomb.
His end was sudden . . . strangely so;
Osiris stalks our land. Kamphé and little Ti (his daugh-
ter—wife)
Both dead within a week. Ah me, I fear
Some priestly treachery; but see! What crouching shape
is this? . . . Peace, fool! "

39

" *I did not speak . . . Oh, Queen.*"

" *ENOUGH. Thou weariest me.*"

" *I go!* "

" *Yet stay! Where is thy Lord?* "

" *Alas! I do not know.*"

" *Then get ye gone—from hence!* "

" *I shall obey.*"

" . . . Wail it! " Mrs. Mary rested.

" Wail what, Mrs. Mary? "

" Let me hear that *bey*: O-bey. Sound your menace."

" I shall o-bey."

" *O beating heart,*" Mrs. Mary paced stormily the room, "*Tumultuous throbbing breast. Alas! how art thou laden? . . .*"

She turned.

" Slave! "

" Me, Mrs. Mary? "

" Come on. Come on."

" Slave's off."

" Pst, girl. Then take *the Duke!* "

" *Fairest——*"

" *High Horus! . . . What! Back from Ethiopia and the Nubian Army! Is't indeed Ismenias . . .?* "

" *Listen.*"

" *Hast deserted Ptolemy?* "

" *Fairest——*"

" *O Gods of Egypt——*"

" Some one wants you, Mrs. Mary."

" Wants me? "

" Your chauffeur, I think."

" The car, M'm," a servant announced.

" Ah!" she broke off. " An engagement, I fear. But come and see me again. Come one day to the theatre. Our stage-door is in Sloop Street, an *impasse* off the Strand." And Mrs. Mary, gathering up her skirts, nodded and withdrew.

" BLACK her great boots! Not I," Miss Sinquier said to herself as she turned her back on Mary Lodge to wend her way westward across the Park.

She was to meet Mrs. Sixsmith at a certain club on Hay Hill towards dusk to learn whether any tempting offer had been submitted Sir Oliver for her pearls.

" If I chose I suppose I could keep them," she murmured incoherently to herself as she crossed the Row.

It was an airless afternoon.

Under the small formal trees sheltering the path she clapped her sunshade to, and slackened speed.

The rhododendrons, in vivid clumps of new and subtle colours brushing the ground, were in their pride. Above, the sky showed purely blue. She walked on a little way towards Stanhope Gate, when, overcome by the odoriferous fragrance of heliotropes and xenias, she sank serenely to a bench.

Far off by the Serpentine a woman was preaching from a tree to a small audience gathered beneath. How primeval she looked as her arms shot out in argument, a discarded cock's-feather boa looped to an upper bough dangling like some dark python in the air above.

Miss Sinquier sat on until the shadows fell.

She found her friend on reaching Hay Hill in the midst of muffins and tea.

" I gave you up. I thought you lost," Mrs. Sixsmith exclaimed, hitching higher her veil with fingers super-manicured, covered in oxydised metal rings.

" I was dozing in the Park."

" Dreamy kid."

" On my back neck I've such a freckle."

" Did you see Mammy Mary? "

" I did."

" Well? "

" Nothing; she offered me Miss Jacks' leavings."

" Not good enough."

" What of Sir Oliver? "

" I hardly know how to tell you."

" Has he——? "

Mrs. Sixsmith nodded.

" He has had an offer of two thousand pounds," she triumphantly said, " for the pearls alone."

" Two thousand pounds! "

" Call it three o's."

" Okh! "

" Consider what commercial credit that means. . . ."

" I shall play Juliet."

" Juliet? "

" I shall have a season."

" Let me take the theatre for you."

" Is it a dream? "

" I will find you actors—great artists."

" Oh, God! "

" And, moreover, I have hopes for the silver too. Sir Oliver is enchanted with the spoons—the Barnabas spoon especially. He said he had never seen a finer. Such a beautiful little Barny, such a rapture of a little sinner as it is, in every way."

Miss Sinquier's eyes shone.

" I'll have that boy."

" What—what boy? "

" Harold Weathercock."

" You desire him? "

" To be my Romeo, of course."

" It depends if the Dream will release him."

" It must! It shall! "

" I'll peep in on him and sound him, if you like."

" We'll go together."

" Very well."

" Do you know where he lives? "

" In Foreign-Colony Street. He and a friend of his, Noel Nice, share a studio there. Not to paint in, alas! It's to wash."

" What? "

" They've made a little laundry of it. And when they're not acting actually, they wash. Oh! sometimes when Mr. Nice spits across his iron and says Pah! it makes one ill."

" Have they any connection? "

Mrs. Sixsmith bent her eyes to her dress.

" Mr. Sixsmith often sent them things . . . little things," she said. " His linen was his pride. You might annex him, perhaps. He's played Mercutio before."

" Is he handsome? "

" Paul? He's more interesting than handsome. *Unusual*, if you know . . ."

" What *did* you do to separate? "

" I believe I bit him."

" You did! "

" He ran at me with the fire-dogs first."

" I suppose you annoyed him? "

" The cur! "

" Something tells me you're fond of him still."

From her reticule Mrs. Sixsmith took a small note-book and made an entry therein.

" . . . The divine Shakespeare! " she sighed.

" I mean to make a hit with him."

" Listen to me."

" Well? "

" My advice to you is, hire a playhouse—the Cobbler's End, for example—for three round months at a reasonable rent, with a right, should you wish, to sub-let."

" It's so far off."

" Define ' far off.' "

" Blackfriars Bridge."

" I've no doubt by paying a fortune you could find a more central position if you care to wait. The Bolivar Theatre, possibly——; or the Cone . . . At the Cone there's a joy-plank from the auditorium to the stage, so that, should you want to ever, you can come right out into the stalls."

" I want my season at once," Miss Sinquier said.

Mrs. Sixsmith toyed with her rings.

" What do you say," she asked, " to making an informal début (before ' royal ' auspices!) at the Esmé Fisher ' Farewell ' coming off next week? "

" Why not! "

" Some of the stage's brightest ornaments have consented to appear."

" I'd like particulars."

" I'll send a note to the secretary, Miss Willinghorse, straight away," Mrs. Sixsmith murmured, gathering up her constant Juno beneath her arm, and looking about her for some ink.

" Send it later, from the Café Royal."

" I can't go any more to the Café Royal," Mrs. Sixsmith said. " I owe money there . . . To all the waiters."

" Wait till after we've seen the Washingtons."

" The Washingtons? Who are they? "

" Don't you know? "

" Besides, I've a small headache," Mrs. Sixsmith said, selecting herself a quill.

" What can I do to relieve it? " Miss Sinquier wondered, taking up a newspaper as her friend commenced to write.

Heading the agony list some initials caught her eye.

" S——h S——r. Come back. All shall be forgiven," she read.

" I can't epistolise while you make those *unearthly* noises," Mrs. Sixsmith complained.

" I didn't mean to."

" Where are we going to dine? "

" Where is there wonderful to go? "

" How about a grill? "

" I don't mind."

" The Piccadilly? We're both about got up for it."

Miss Sinquier rolled her eyes.

" The Grill-room at the Piccadilly isn't going to cure a headache," she remarked.

X

To watch Diana rise blurred above a damp chemise from a fifth-floor laundry garden in Foreign-Colony Street, Soho, had brought all Chelsea (and part of Paris) to study illusive atmospherical effects from the dizzy drying-ground of those versatile young men Harold Weathercock and Noel Nice.

Like a necropolis at the Resurrection, or some moody vision of Blake, would it appear under the evanescent rays of the moon.

Nighties, as evening fell, would go off into proud Praxiteles-torsos of Nymphs or Muses: pants and ready-mades, at a hint of air, would pirouette and execute a phantom ballet from Don John.

Beyond the clothes-lines was a Pagoda, set up in an extravagant mood, containing a gilded Buddha—a thorn and a symbol of unrighteousness to a convent of Ursulines whose recreation yard was underneath.

Here, at a certain hour when the Mother Superior was wont to walk round and round her preserves, a young, bewhiskered man frequently would come bearing ceremonial offerings of rice or linen newly washed, and falling flat before the shrine would roll himself about and beat the ground as if in mortal anguish of his sins before her fascinated eye. Here, too, from time to time, festivities would take place—sauteries (to a piano-organ), or convivial *petits soupers* after the play.

An iron ladder connected the roof with the work-rooms and living-rooms below.

Ascending this by the light of the stars, Mrs. Six-smith and the *New Juliet*, gay from a certain grill, audaciously advanced, their playful screams rendered inaudible by the sounds of a tricksome waltz wafted down to them from the piano-organ above.

Items of linen nestling close to a line overhead showed palely against the night like roosting doves.

" Help . . . Oh! she's falling," Mrs. Sixsmith screamed. " Are you there, Mr. Nice? "

" Give me your hand," Miss Sinquier begged.

" Should she rick her spine . . ."

" Whew-ps! " Miss Sinquier exclaimed, scrambling to the top.

London, beyond the frail filigree cross on the Ursulines' bleached wall, blazed with light. From the Old Boar and Castle over the way came a perfect flood of it. And all along the curved river-line from Westminster to St. Paul's glittered lamps, lamps, lamps.

Folding an arm about her friend's " wasp " waist, Mrs. Sixsmith whirled her deftly round to a wild street air:

> " I like your ways,
> I like your style,
> You are my darling——"

she hummed as the organ stopped.

" Come to finish the evening? "

A small, thick-set, grizzled man with dark æsthetic eyes and a pinkish nose, the result maybe of continuously tinting it for music-hall purposes, addressed the breathless ladies in a broad, inquiring voice.

" Is that *you*, Mr. Smee? " Mrs. Sixsmith asked, surprised.

" Call me ' Shawn.' "

" We've only come on business."

" Don't! You make me laf."

" Then—do it," Mrs. Sixsmith serenely said, resting her left knee against an empty beer keg

" They're not back from the theatre yet."

47

" Turn for us till they come."

Mr. Smee dashed from a crimpled brow a wisp of drooping hair.

" By your leave, ladies," he said, " I'll just slip across to the Old Boar and Castle and sample a snack at the bar."

" Don't run off, Mr. Smee. You really mustn't. On tiles, they say, one usually meets with *cats*."

" Oh, my word."

Mrs. Sixsmith placed a hand to her hip in the style of an early John.

" How long is it—say—since we met? " she inquired. " Not since my wedding, I do believe."

" What's become of those kiddy bridesmaids you had? " Mr. Smee warily asked.

" Gerty Gale and Joy Patterson?—I'm sure I don't know."

" Oh, my word!"

" Well, how goes the world with *you*, Mr. Smee? "

" So-so. I've been away on tour. Mildred Milson and Co. Oh! my Lord—it was. No sooner did we get to Buxton—down in Derbyshire—than Miss Milson fell sick and had to be left behind."

" What was wrong with her? "

" Exposure . . . On Bank Holiday some of the company hired a three-horse char-à-banc and drove from Buxton over to Castleton Caves—my hat. What hills!—and from there we went to take a squint at Chatsworth, where Miss Milson came over queer."

" And how does Mrs. Smee? "

" So-so."

" One never sees her now."

" There she sits all day, reading Russian novels. Talk of gloom! "

" Really? "

" Oh, it is! "

" Well . . . I'm fond of thoughtful, theosophical

reading, too, Mr. Smee," Mrs. Sixsmith said. "Madame Blavatsky and Mrs. Annie Besant are both favourites with me."

Mr. Smee jerked an eloquent thumb.

" Who have you brought along? "

" She's a special pal of mine."

" Married? "

" Mon Dieu," Mrs. Sixsmith doubtfully said. " Je crois que c'est une Pucelle."

" Never! " Mr. Smee, completely mystified, hazarded.

" Fie donc. Comme c'est méchant."

" Wee, wee."

Mrs. Sixsmith tittered.

" She's going into management very soon."

" Swank? "

" We seek a Romeo, Mr. Smee."

" Now, now! . . . "

" Don't look like that, Mr. Smee—nobody's asking you," Mrs. Sixsmith murmured.

Mr. Smee scratched reflectively his head.

" Who is it you're after? " he asked.

" We fancied Mr. Weathercock might suit."

" God has given him looks, but no brains," Mr. Smee emphatically declared. " No more brains than a cow in a field."

" His is indeed a charming face," Mrs. Sixsmith sighed. " And as to his brains, Mr. Smee—why, come! "

" Who's to create the countess? " he asked.

" Lady Capulet? It's not determined yet."

" Why not canvass the wife? "

" Has she been in Shakespeare before? "

" From the time she could toddle; in *A Midsummer-Night's Dream*, when not quite two, she was the Bug with gilded wings."

" Pet! "

" Sure . . ."

Mrs. Sixsmith clasped prayerfully her hands.

" And in Mr. Smee," she said, " I see the makings of a fine Friar Lawrence! "

" How's that? "

" With a few choice *concetti*."

" Faith! "

" I see the lonely cell, the chianti-flask, the crucifix . . ."

" Gosh! "

" I see Verona . . . the torrid sky . . . the town ascending, up, up, up. I hear the panting nurse. She knocks. Your priest's eyes glisten. She enters, blouse-a-gape—a thorough coster. You raise your cowl . . . Chianti? She shakes her head. Benedictine? No! no! A little Chartreuse, then? Certainly not! Nothing . . . You squeeze her waist. Her cries ' go through ' Lady Capulet and her daughter in the distant city on their way to mass. Romeo enters. So! " Mrs. Sixsmith broke off as Mr. Weathercock and a curly-headed lad, followed by a swathed woman and a whey-faced child, showed themselves upon the stairs.

Mrs. Sixsmith sought Miss Sinquier's arm.

" Listen to me, my darling! " she said.

" Well? "

" Write."

" What? "

" Write."

" Why? "

" Because I fear we intrude."

"Intrude?" Harold Weathercock exclaimed, coming up. " I assure you it's a treat . . ."

Mrs. Sixsmith threw a sidelong, intriguing glance across her shoulder.

" Who's the cure in plaits? " she demanded.

" It's Little Mary Mant—she's seeing her sister home."

" Oh! . . . Is that Ita? " Mrs. Sixsmith murmured, stepping forward to embrace Miss " Ita Iris " of the Dream.

Miss Sinquier swooped.

" I'm having a season, she, without further pre-amble, began. " And I want to persuade you to join——"

" Principal? "

" Yes."

" I should like to play for you," Mr. Weathercock said.

" Harold! "

Miss Mant addressed him softly.

" Well? "

" Honey husband . . ."

" Hook it! "

" Give me a cigarette."

" Mary! " her sister called.

" Quick! 'cos of Ita."

" Mary Mant."

Miss Mant tossed disdainfully an ultra-large and pasty-faced head.

" Why must you insult me, Ita? " she bitterly asked. " You *know* I'm Miss Iris."

" I know you're Miss Mant."

" No, I'm not."

" Yes, you are."

" No, I'm *not*."

" I tell you, you are! "

" Liar! "

" M-A-N-T! "

" Oh, stow it," Mr. Smee said. " Put it by."

" I'm Réné Iris."

" Réné Rats."

Mrs. Sixsmith looked detached.

" Is that a wash-tub? " she asked.

" Certainly."

" What's that odd thing floating, like the ghost of a child unborn? "

" It belongs to Mrs. Mary."

" There's a rumour—she refuses a fortune to show herself in Revue."

" With her hearse-horse tread . . ."

" Sh—— Harold worships her."

" Oh, no."

" He sees things in her that we don't, perhaps."

" To some ideas," Mrs. Sixsmith said, " I suppose she's very blooming still . . ."

" If it wasn't for her figure, which is really a disgrace."

Miss Iris smiled.

She had a tired mouth, contrasting vividly with the artificial freshness of her teeth.

" When I reach my zenith," she declared, " it's Farewell."

" Shall you assist at poor Esmé Fisher's? "

" A couple of songs—that's all."

Mrs. Sixsmith looked away.

" Naturally," Miss Sinquier was saying, " one can't expect instantly to be a draw. More than—perhaps—just a little! "

"With a man who understands in the Box Office . . ."

" Some one with a big nose and a strong will, eh? "

Mr. Nice lifted a rusty iron and wiped it across his leg.

" In my opinion," he said, " to associate oneself with a sanctified classic is a huge mistake. And why start a season on the tragic tack? "

" Because——"

" Suppose it's a frost? "

" Oh! "

" Suppose your venture fails. Suppose the thing's a drizzle."

" What then? "

"There's a light comedy of mine that should suit you."

" Of yours! "

" Appelled *Sweet Maggie Maguire*."

" Tell me why she was sweet, Mr. Nice," Mrs. Sixsmith begged.

" Why she was sweet? I really don't know."

" Was she sentimental? . . . "

" She was an invalid. A bed-ridden beauty . . . and, of course, the hero's a Doctor."

" Oh! my word! "

" Is there anyone at home? " A tired voice came thrilling up from below.

" Who comes? "

Mrs. Sixsmith started.

" It sounds to me like my husband," she said, with an involuntary nervous movement of the hands.

" I forgot," Mr. Weathercock said. " He mentioned he might blow in."

" Oh! "

" I'd take to my heels! " Miss Iris advised.

Mrs. Sixsmith stood transfixed.

The moonlight fell full on her, making her feature look drawn and haggard.

X I

LIKE wildfire the rumour ran. The King had knighted
—he had knighted—by what accident?—Mr. Mary,
in lieu of Mr. Fisher, at Mr. Fisher's own farewell. In
the annals of the stage such an occurrence was unheard
of, unique.

The excitement in the green-room was intense.

" M-m! He is not de first to zell 'is birs-r-rite for a
mess of porridge! " Yvonde Yalta, the playgoers'
darling, remarked as she poised with an extravagant
play of arms, a black glittering bandeau on her short
flaxen hair.

" A mess of pottage! " some one near her said.

" You correct me? Ah, sanx! I am so grateful, so—
so grateful," the charming creature murmured as she
sailed away.

From the auditorium came a suppressed titter.

The curtain had risen some few minutes since on
Mlle. Fanfette and Monsieur Coquelet de Chausse-
pierre of the Théâtre Sans Rancune in the comedietta,
Sydney, or There's No Resisting Him.

" It's extraordinary I've never seen a man knighted,"
a show-girl twittered, " and I've seen a good deal
. . ."

" How do they do them? "

" Like this," a sparkling brunette answered, be-
stowing a sly pat on the interlocutress with the back
of a brush.

" Of all the common——! "

" Ladies! Ladies! "

" Who was in front at the time? "

"I was!" Mrs. Sixsmith said, who had just peeped in to exchange a few words with her friend.

"You were?"

"I was selling sweets in the vestibule and saw it all. Really! If I live to be an old woman I shan't forget it. Mr. Mary—*Sir Maurice*—was in the lobby chatting with Sylvester Fry of the *Dispatch*, when the Royal party arrived. The King instantly noticed him and sent one of his suite, quite unpremeditatedly, it seemed, to summon him, and in a trice . . . Oh! . . . and I *never* saw the Queen look so charming. She has a gold dress turning to white through the most exquisite gradations . . ."

Mrs. Sixsmith was overcome.

"A-wheel," Miss Sinquier's dresser disrespectfully said, "how was the poor man to tell? Both the blighters—God forgive me—are equally on their last legs."

Miss Sinquier shivered.

"Is it a good house?" she inquired.

"Splendid! Outside they're flying five 'full' boards . . . There's not a single vacant place. Poor Sydney Iphis gave half a guinea for a seat in the slips."

"Are you here all alone?"

"I'm with Sir Oliver Dawtry," Mrs. Sixsmith replied, "except when I'm running about! . . . Can I sell anyone anything?" she inquired, raising sonorously her voice. "Vanilla! Caramel! Chocolate! . . . Comfits!" she warbled.

"What have you netted?"

"Eighteenpence only, so far;—from such an angel!"

"Comfits, did you say?" a round-faced, piquant little woman asked.

"Despite disguise! If it isn't Arthurine Smee!"

The actress displayed astonishment.

Nature had thrown up upon her lip and cheek two big blonde moles that procured for her physiognomy, somehow or other, an unusual degree of expression.

"My husband has been waiting to hear from you," she said, " as agent to this *Miss Sin*——, the new star with the naughty name, and from all I could make out I understand it would be likely to be a *Double Engagement*."

"This is Miss Sinquier," Mrs. Sixsmith exclaimed. Miss Sinquier blinked.

"Have you done it much?" she asked.

"Often."

"Where?"

"Everywhere."

"For example?"

"I may say I've played Pauline and Portia and Puck . . ."

"Mother-to-Juliet I fear's the best I've to offer."

Mrs. Smee consulted enigmatically the nearest mole in reach of her tongue.

"Were I to play her in ' good preservation,' " she inquired, " I suppose there'd be no objection?"

"Why, none!"

"Just a girlish touch . . ."

"Mrs. Smee defies time," Mrs. Sixsmith remarked.

"My dear, I once was thought to be a very pretty woman. . . . All I can do now is to urge my remains."

Miss Sinquier raised a forefinger.

Voices shivering in altercation issued loudly from a private dressing-room next door.

"What's up?"

"Oh, dear! Oh, dear!" the wardrobe-mistress, entering, said. "Sir Maurice and Mr. Fisher are passing sharp words with a couple of pitchforks."

"What!"

"The ' Farm-players ' sent them over from the Bolivar for their Pig-sty scene—and now poor Mr. Mary, *Sir M'riss*, and Mr. Fisher are fighting it out, and Mrs. Mary, *her ladyship*, has joined the struggle."

" Murder! " called a voice.

" Glory be to God."

Mrs. Sixsmith rolled her eyes.

" Da! " she gasped, as Lady Mary, a trifle dazed
but decked in smiles, came bustling in.

" Oh, Men! Men! Men! " she exclaimed, going off
into a hearty laugh. " Rough angelic brutes! . . ."

She was radiant.

She had a gown of shot brocade, a high lace ruff
and a silver girdle of old German work that had an
ivory missal falling from it.

" Quarrelsome, quarrelling kings," she stuttered,
drifting towards a toilet-table—the very one before
which Miss Sinquier was making her face.

On all sides from every lip rose up a chorus of
congratulations.

" Viva, Lady Mary! "

Touched, responsive, with a gesture springing
immediately from the heart, the consummate Victorian
extended impulsive happy hands.

" God bless you, dears," she said.

" Three cheers for Lady Mary! "

The illustrious woman quashed a tear.

" Am I white behind? " she asked.

" Allow me, milady," the wardrobe-mistress
wheezed.

" I fancy I heard a rip! . . ."

" There must have been quite a scrimmage."

From the orchestra a melodious throb-thrum-
hrob told a " curtain."

" Lady Mary—*you*, Mum," a call-boy chirped.

" Me? "

" Five minutes."

Lady Mary showed distress.

"For goodness sake, my dear," she addressed Miss
Sinquier, "do leave yourself alone. I want the glass."

But Miss Sinquier seemed engrossed.

At her elbow a slip of a " Joy-baby " was holding forth with animation to Mrs. Sixsmith and Mrs. Smee.

" That was one of my dreams," she was saying, " and last night again I had another—in spite of a night-light, too! It began by a ring formed of crags and boulders enclosing a troop of deer—oh, such a herd of them—delicate, distinguished animals with little pom-pom horns, and some had poodles' tails. Sitting behind a rhododendron bush was an old gentleman on a white horse; he never moved a muscle. Suddenly I became aware of a pack of dogs . . . And then, before my very eyes, one of the dogs transformed itself into a giraffe . . ."

" You must have been out to supper."

" It's true I had. Oh, it was a merry meal."

" Who gave it? "

" Dore Davis did: to meet her betrothed—Sir Francis Four."

" What's he like? "

" Don't ask me. It makes one tired to look at him."

" Was it a party? "

" Nothing but literary-people with their Beatrices . . . My dear *the scum!* Half-way through supper Dore got her revolver out and began shooting the glass drops off her chandelier."

" I should like to see her trousseau," Mrs. Sixsmith sighed.

" It isn't up to much. Anything good she sells—on account of bailiffs."

" Pooh! She should treat them all *en reine*."

Mrs. Smee looked wise.

" Always be civil with bailiffs," she said; " never ruffle them! If you queen a sheriff's officer remember there's no getting rid of him. He clings on—like a poor relation."

" Oh, well," Mrs. Sixsmith replied, " I always treat

the worms *en reine;* not," she added wittily, " that I
ever have . . ."

Miss Sinquier twirled herself finally about.

" There," she murmured, " I'm going out into the
wings."

" When's your call? "

" After Lady Mary."

For her unofficial first appearance she was resolved
to woo the world with a dance—a dance all fearless
somersaults and quivering *battements;* a young Hun-
garian meanwhile recording her movements sensitively
upon a violin.

She was looking well in an obedient little ballet
skirt that made action a delight. Her hair, piled high
in a towering toupee, had a white flower in it.

" Down a step and through an arch." A pierrette
who passed her in the corridor directed her to the
stage.

It was Miss Ita Iris of the Dream.

Miss Sinquier tingled.

How often on the cold flags of the great church at
home had she asked the way before!

" O Lord," she prayed now, " let me conquer.
Let me! Amen."

She was in the wings.

Above her, stars sparkled lavishly in a darkling sky,
controlled by a bare-armed mechanic who was en-
deavouring, it seemed, to deliver himself of a moon;
craning from a ladder at the risk of his life, he pushed
it gently with a big soft hand.

Miss Sinquier turned her eyes to the stage.

The round of applause accorded Lady Mary on her
entry was gradually dying away.

From her shelter Miss Sinquier could observe her,
in opulent silhouette, perfectly at her ease.

She stood waiting for the last huzzas to subside
with bowed head and folded hands—like some great

sinner—looking reverently up through her eyelashes at the blue silk hangings of the Royal box.

By degrees all clatter ceased.

Approaching the footlights with a wistful smile, the favourite woman scanned the stalls.

" Now most of you here this afternoon," she intimately began, " I will venture to say, never heard of Judy Jacock. I grant you, certainly, there's nothing very singular in that; for her life, which was a strangely frail one, essentially was obscure. Judy herself was *obscure* . . . And so that is why I say you can't have ever heard of her! . . . Because she was totally unknown. . . . Ah, poor wee waif! alas, she's dead now. Judy's among the angels . . . and the beautiful little elegy which, with your consent, I intend forthwith to submit, is written around her, around little Judy, and around her old Father, her ' *Da* '—James, who was a waiter. And while he was away waiting one day—he used to wipe the plates on the seat of his breeches!—his little Judy died. Ah, poor old James. Poor Sir James. But let the poet," she broke off suddenly, confused, " take up the tale himself, or, rather —to be more specific!—*herself*. For the lines that follow, which are *inédits*, are from the seductive and charming pen of Lady Violet Sleepwell."

Lady Mary coughed, winked archly an eye, and began quite carelessly as if it were Swinburne:

" I never *knew* James Jacock's child . . .
I knew he *had* a child!
The daintiest little fairy that ever a father knew.
She was all contentment . . ."

Miss Sinquier looked away.

To her surprise, lurking behind a property torso of " a Faun," her pigtails roped with beads of scarlet glass, was Miss May Mant.

" Tell me what you are up to? " she asked.

" Sh——! Don't warn Ita! "

" Why should I? "

" I dodged her. Beautifully."

" What for? "

" If she thought I was going on the stage, she'd be simply wild."

" Are you? "

" I intend tacking on in the Pope's Procession."

" That won't be just yet."

" Oh, isn't it wonderful? "

" What? "

" Being here."

" It's rather pleasant."

" Can you feel the boards? "

" A little."

" They go *right* through me. Through my shoes, up my legs, and at my heart they sting."

" Kiss me."

" I love you."

" Pet."

" Do I look interesting? "

" Ever so."

" Would you take me for a Cardinal's comfort? "

Lady Mary lifted up her voice:

" Come, Judy, the angel said,
And took her from her little bed,
And through the air they quickly sped
Until they reached God's throne;
So, there, they dressed her all in white,
They say she was a perfect sight,
Celestial was her mien! "

" Lady Violet Sleepwell admires Ita."

" Indeed."

" She's a victim to chloral."

" Rose-coiffed stood J.
      Amid the choir,
      Celestial-singing! "

The august artiste glowed.

" Ita thinks she drinks."

" I shouldn't wonder," Miss Sinquier replied, covering her face with her hands.

Through her fingers she could contemplate her accompanist's lanky figure as he stood in the opposite wing busily powdering his nose.

The moment, it seemed, had come.

Yet not quite—the public, who loved tradition, was determined on obtaining an encore.

Lady Mary was prepared to acquiesce.

Curtseying from side to side and wafting kisses to the gods, she announced:

" The Death of Hortense; by *Desire*."

XII

The Source Theatre.

DEAR MOTHER,—I saw your notice in a newspaper not very long ago, and this morning I came across it again in the *Dispatch*. Really I don't know what there can be to " forgive," and as to " coming back! "— I have undertaken the management of this theatre, where rehearsals of *Romeo and Juliet* have already begun. This is the little house where Audrey Anderson made her début, and where Avize Mendoza made such a hit. You could imagine nothing cosier or more intimate if you tried. Father would be charmed (tell him, for, of course, he sometimes speaks of me in the long *trifle* evenings as he smokes a pipe) with the foyer, which has a mural design in marquetry, showing Adam and Eve in the Garden of Eden, sunning themselves by the side of a well. They say the theatre contains a well *beneath the stage*, which is why it's known as the Source. I have left, I'm glad to say, the hotel, which was getting dreadfully on my nerves, for a dressing-room here, where I pass the nights now: an arrangement that suits me, as I like to be on the spot. A sister of Ita Iris of the Dream Theatre keeps me company, so that I'm not a bit solitary. We understand each other to perfection, and I find her helpful to me in many ways. She is such an affectionate child, and I do not think I shall regret it. I've decided to have half my teeth taken out by a man in Knightsbridge—some trial to me, I fear; but, alas, we've all to carry our cross! I seem to have nothing but debts. Clothes, *as well* as scenery, would ruin anyone.

I'm allotting a little box to you and father for the opening night, unless you would prefer two stalls?

The other afternoon I " offered my services " and obtained three curtains at a gala matinée; I wish you could have been at it!

Your devoted Daughter.

I went to the oratory on Sunday; it was nothing but a blaze of candles.

Remember me to Leonard and Gripper—also Kate.

XIII

An absence of ventilation made the room an oven and discouraged sleep. Through the width of skylight, in inert recumbence, she could follow wonderingly the frail pristine tints of dawn. Flushed, rose-barred, it spread above her with fantastic drifting clouds masking the morning stars.

From a neighbouring church a clock struck five.

Miss Sinquier sighed; she had not closed her eyes the whole night through.

" One needs a blind," she mused, " and a pane——"

She looked about her for something to throw.

Cinquecento Italian things—a chest, a crucifix, a huge guitar, a grim carved catafalque all purple sticks and violet legs (Juliet's) crowded the floor.

" A mess of glass . . . and cut my feet . . ." she murmured, gathering about her a *négligé* of oxydised knitted stuff and sauntering out towards the footlights in quest of air.

Notwithstanding the thermometer, she could hear Miss May Mant breathing nasally from behind her door.

The stage was almost dark.

" Verona," set in autumn trees, looked fast asleep. Here and there a campanile shot up, in high relief, backed by a scenic hill, or an umbrella-pine. On a column in the " Market Place " crouched a brazen lion.

An acrobatic impulse took her at the sight of it.

> " Sono pazza per te
> *Si!* Sono pazza, pazza, pazza . . .
> Pazza per amore,"

she warbled, leaping lightly over the footlights into the stalls.

The auditorium, steeped in darkness, felt extinguished, chill.

Making a circuit of the boxes, she found her way up a stairway into the promenade.

Busts of players, busts of poets, busts of peris, interspersed by tall mirrors in gilt-bordered mouldings, smiled on her good-day.

Sinking to a low, sprucely-cushioned seat, she breathed a sigh of content.

Rid of the perpetual frictions of the inevitable *personnel*, she could possess the theatre, for a little while, in quietude to herself.

In the long window boxes, tufts of white daisies inclining to the air brought back to mind a certain meadow, known as *Basings*, a pet haunt with her at home.

At the pond end, in a small coppice, doves cried " Coucoussou-coucoussou " all the day long.

Here, soon a year ago, while weaving herself a garland (she was playing at being Europa with the Saunders' Fifeshire bull; flourishing flowers at it; tempting it with waving poppies; defying it to bear her away from the surrounding stagnance), the realisation of her dramatic gift first discovered itself.

And then, her thoughts tripped on, *he* came, the Rev. George—" just as I was wondering to whom to apply "—and drew all Applethorp to St. Ann-on-the-Hill by the persuasive magnetism of his voice; largely due—so he said—to " scientific production." To the *Bromley Breath!* He never could adequately thank Elizabeth, Mrs. Albert Bromley, for all she had done. No; because words failed . . . Her Institute, for him, would be always " top-o'-the-tree," and when asked, by her, " What tree ? " he had answered with a cryptic look: " She trains them for the stage."

Dear heart! How much he seemed to love 'it. He had known by their green-room names all the leading stars, and could tell, on occasion, little anecdotes of each.

It was he who narrated how Mrs. Mary (as she was then), on the first night of *Gulnara, Queen of the Lattermonians*, got caught in the passenger-lift on the way from her dressing-room to the stage and was obliged to allow her understudy to replace her, which with the utmost *éclat* she did, while Mrs. Mary, who could overhear the salvos from her prison, was driven quite distraught at a triumph that, but for the irony of things, would most certainly have been hers.

Miss Sinquier sighed.

" Which reminds me," she murmured, fixing her eyes upon the storied ceiling, " that I've no one at all, should anything happen to me."

She lay back and considered the inchoate imagery painted in gouache above her.

Hydropic loves with arms outstretched in invitation, ladies in hectic hats and billowing silks, courtiers, lap-dogs, peacocks, etc., all intermingled in the pleasantest way.

As she gazed a great peace fell upon her. Her eyelids closed.

. . . .

" Breakfast! "

Miss May Mant woke her with a start.

" Oh ! "

" I laid it to-day in the stalls. "

" Extraordinary child."

" Crumbs in the boxes, I've noticed, encourage mice. . . . They must come from the spring, I think, under the stage."

" One ought to set a trap! "

" Poor creatures . . . they enjoy a good play, I expect, as much as we do," Miss Mant murmured,

setting down the kettle she was holding and lowering
her cheek graciously for a kiss.

" Well? "

" You were asleep."

" Was I horrid? "

" You looked too perfectly orchidaceous."

" Orchidaceous? "

" Like the little women of Outa-Maro."

Miss Sinquier sat up.

" What is there for breakfast?" she asked.

" Do you like porridge? "

" Oh, Réné! "

Miss Mant raised a bare shoulder and crushed it to
an ear.

" Really," she remarked, " I'm at a loss to know
what to give you, Sally; I sometimes ask my self what
Juliet took . . ."

" Why, potions."

" *Ita* takes tea luke with a lemon; and it makes her
so cross."

" Disgusting."

" À la Russe."

" Is she still away? "

" Yes . . . She writes from a toy bungalow, she
says, with the sea at the very door and a small ship-
wreck lying on the beach."

" What of Paris? "

" I'm Page to him, you said so! "

" With her consent."

" Oh, Ita hates the stage. She's only *on it* of course
to make a match . . . she could have been an Irish
countess had she pleased, only she said it wasn't smart
enough, and it sounded too Sicilian."

" Everyone can't be Roman."

" . . . Oh, she's such a minx! In her letter she writes,
' I don't doubt you'll soon grow tired of the Sally-Sin
Theatre and of dancing attendance on the Fair Sink.' "

" Cat."

" And her Manting ways just to annoy. Mant, Mant, Mant! She does it to humiliate. Whenever the Tirds are in earshot she's sure to begin."

" The Tirds? "

" Llewellyn and Lydia. Lydia Tird has an understanding with my big brother. Poor lad! Just before I left home he took the name of Isadore: Isadore Iris. Oh, when Ita heard! Bill Mant she said and made Llewellyn laugh."

" Oh! "

" And now that Mrs. Sixsmith ' Mants ' me almost as much as Ita."

" Why do you dislike her so much? "

" Cadging creature! "

" Réné? "

" Limpet."

" Réné? "

" Parasite."

" Réné——! "

" Scavenger."

" *Basta!* "

" I know all about her."

" What do you know? "

" If I tell you, I'll have to tell you in French."

" Then tell me in French."

" Elle fait les cornes à son mari! "

" What next? "

" She's *divorcée!* "

" Poor soul."

" Out at *Bois St. Jean*—St. John's Wood—she has a villa."

Miss Sinquier got up.

" Anyway," she murmured.

" Oh, Sally . . ."

" Well? "

" You do love me? "

" Why, *of course*."

" Let's go presently to a Turkish bath—after re-hearsal."

" Not to-day."

" . . . Just for a ' Liver Pack '? "

" No."

" Why not? "

" Because . . . and when you're out, don't, dear, forget a mousetrap! "

XIV

To bring together certain of the dramatic critics (such high arbiters of the stage as Sylvester Fry of the *Dispatch*, Lupin Petrol of *Now*, Amethyst Valer of *Fashion*, Berinthia of *Woodfalls*, the terrible, the embittered Berinthia who was also Angela) cards had been sent out from Foreign-Colony Street, in the comprehensive name of Sir Oliver Dawtry, the famous banker and financier, inviting them to meet the new lessee of the Source.

It was one of those sultry summer nights of electricity and tension, when nerves are apt to explode at almost nothing. Beyond the iron Calvary on the Ursulines' great wall, London flared with lights.

Perched upon a parapet in brilliant solitude, her identity unsuspected by the throng, Miss Sinquier, swathed in black mousseline and nursing a sheaf of calla lilies, surveyed the scene with inexpressive eyes.

" And there was the wind bellowing and we witches wailing: and no Macbeth! " a young man with a voice like cheap scent was saying to a sympathetic journalist for whatever it might be worth. . . .

Miss Sinquier craned her head.

Where were the two " Washingtons "? or the little Iris girl?

By the Buddha shrine, festively decked with lamps, couples were pirouetting to a nigger band, while in the vicinity of the buffet a masked adept was holding a clairaudience of a nature only to be guessed at from afar. An agile negro melody, wild rag-time with passages of almost Wesleyan hymnishness—reminiscent of Georgia gospel-missions; the eighteenth century

71

in the Dutch East Indies—charmed and soothed the ear.

Miss Sinquier jigged her foot.

At their cell windows, as if riveted by the lights and commotion, leaned a few pale nuns.

Poor things!

The call of the world could seldom wholly be quenched!

She started as a fan of seabirds' feathers skimmed her arm.

" Sylvester's come," Mrs. Sixsmith in passing said.

" Oh! "

" Aren't you scared? "

" Scared? "

" You know, he always belittles people. Sylvester traduces everyone; he even crabs his daughter; he damns all he sees."

" Boom! "

" How he got up those narrow stairs is a mystery to me." Mrs. Sixsmith smiled.

Miss Sinquier raised her face towards the bustling stars. An elfish horse-shoe moon, felicitously bright, struck her as auspicious.

" One should bow to it," she said.

" Idolatry! "

" There! look what nodding does."

A blanche bacchante with a top-knot of leaves venturesomely approached.

" I'm Amethyst," she murmured.

" Indeed? "

" Of *Fashion*. You are Miss Sinquier, I take it, whose costumes for Romeo—Renaissance, and ergo *à la mode!*—I so long to hear about."

Miss Sinquier dimpled.

" The frocks," she said, " some of them, will be simply killing."

" I want your first."

" Loose white."

" I suppose, *coiffé de sphinx avec un tortis de perles?* "

Miss Sinquier shook her head.

"No ' Juliet-cap' of spurious pearls for me," she said.

" You dare to abolish it? "

" I do."

" You excite me."

" Unless the bloom is off the peach, Juliet needs no nets."

Miss Valer lowered discreetly her voice.

" And your Romeo? " she queried. " He must make love angelically? "

" He does."

" I admire enormously his friend."

" Mr. Nice? "

" He has such perfect sloth. I love his lazaroni-ness, his Riva-degli-Schiavoni-ness . . . He's very, very handsome. But, of course, it cannot last! "

" No? "

" Like an open rose. Have you no sympathy yourself? "

" None."

" That's a pity. An actress . . . she needs a lover: a sort of husbandina, as it were . . . I always say Passion tells: *L'amour!* "

Miss Sinquier threw a glance towards Mrs. Sixsmith, who stood listlessly flirting her fan.

" I'm going to the buffet, child," she said.

" Then I think I'll join you."

And drawing her friend's arm within her own, Miss Sinquier moved away.

" She must belong to more than one weekly! " she reflected.

" You didn't mention your Old Mechlin scarf, or your fox-trimmed nightie," Mrs. Sixsmith murmured, dexterously evading the psychic freedoms of the masked adept.

" Have you no shame, Paul?" she asked.

" Paul! "

Miss Sinquier wondered.

" Mephisto! I know his parlour tricks . . . though it would only be just, perhaps, to say he did foresee our separation some time before it occurred."

" Oh, how extraordinary."

" Once as I was making ready to pay some calls, in order to frighten me, he caused the hare's foot on my toilet-table to leave its carton sheath and go skipping about the room."

" What ever did you do? "

" My dear, I was disgusted. It really seemed as if the whole of Womanhood was outraged. So, to *punish* him—for revenge—instead of going to a number of houses that day, I went to only one."

" There wouldn't be time? "

" I shall always blame myself . . ."

" Why? "

But a lanthorn falling in flames just then above them put an end to the conversation.

" That's the second I've seen drop," Miss May Mant exclaimed, darting up.

" What have you been up to? "

" Having my bumps examined."

" What! "

" By the masked professor . . . Oh, the things he said; only fancy, he told me I'd cause the death of one both near and dear! Ita's near . . . but she certainly isn't dear—odious cat."

" He must have thought you curiously credulous," Miss Sinquier murmured, turning her head aside.

To her annoyance she perceived the scholarly representative of the *Dispatch*—a man of prodigious size —leaning solidly on a gold-headed cane while appraising her to Sir Oliver Dawtry, from her bebandeaued head to her jewelly shoes.

" She reminds me just a little of some one *de l'Évangile!*" she could hear the great critic say.

" Sylvester! "

" Oh? "

" Should he speak," Mrs. Sixsmith murmured, wincing at the summer lightning that flickered every now and then, " don't forget the mediæval nightie or the Mechlin lace! Five long yards—a cloud . . ."

Miss Sinquier buried her lips in her flowers.

Through the barred windows of the convent opposite certain novices appeared to be enjoying a small saltation among themselves.

Up and down the corridor to the yearning melody of the minstrel players they twirled, clinging to one another in an ecstasy of delight.

Her fine eyes looked beautiful as, raising them fraught with soul, they met the veteran critic's own.

X V

" O, DEAR God, help me. Hear me, Jesu. Hear me and forgive me and be offended not if what I ask is vain . . . soften all hostile hearts and let them love me—adore me!—O Heaven, help me to please. Vouchsafe at each *finale* countless curtains; and in the ' Potion Scene,' O Lord, pull me through . . ."

Unwilling to genuflect in the presence of her maid, who would interpret any unwontedness of gesture as first-night symptoms of fear, Miss Sinquier lifted her face towards the bluish light of day that filtered obliquely through the long glass-plating above.

" There's a cat on the skylight, Smith," was what she said as her maid with a telegram recalled her wandering gaze to earth.

It was a telegram from her father.

" Missed conveyance York," she read. " Bishop-thorpe to-night archiepiscopal blessings."

" Ah, well . . ." she professionally philosophised, " there'll be *deadheads* besides, I've no doubt."

" Any answer, miss? "

" Go, Smith, to the box office, and say G 2 and 3 (orchestra) have been returned; there's no answer," she added, moving towards the brightly lit dressing-room beyond.

Ensconced in an easy chair, before a folding mirror that, rich in reflections, encompassed her screen-like about, sat Mrs. Sixsmith pensively polishing her nails.

Miss Sinquier bit her lip.

" I thought——" she began.

" Sh——! Be Juliet now. We're in Verona," Mrs. Sixsmith exclaimed. " *Fuori* the doors."

" Fancy finding *you*."

" Me? "

" What are you doing in *my Italy?* "

Mrs. Sixsmith threw a glance at herself in the glass.
" I'm a girl friend," she said; " a Venetian acquaint-
ance: someone *Julie* met while paddling in the Adriatic
—in fact, *cara cuore*, I'm a daughter of the Doge. Yes;
I'm one of the Dolfin-Trons."

" Don't be ridiculous."

" I'm Catarina Dolfin-Tron."

" Kitty Tron! "

" Your own true Kate."

" When are you going round? "

" Let me finish my hands. My manicurist has left
me with such claws. . . . Poor little soul! When she
came to my wedding-finger she just twiddled her rasp
and broke out crying. ' To be filing people's nails,' she
said, ' while my husband is filing a petition! ' "

" Wonderful that she could."

" This city has its sadness. Your maid, Smith, while
you were in the other room, said, ' Oh, marm, what
you must have endured; *one Smith* was enough for
me.' "

" Poor Kate! "

" Ah, Julie . . ." Mrs. Sixsmith sighed, when the
opening of the door gently was followed by the entry
of Mrs. Smee.

" Am I disturbing you? " she asked.

" No, come in."

" I want to tell you my husband isn't himself."

" He's ill? "

" He's not himself."

" In what way? "

" It's a hard thing for a wife to confess. But for a
première he's nearly always in wine."

" Is he . . . *much?* "

" I never knew him like it! "

77

Mrs. Sixsmith examined her nails.

" So violent? " she ventured.

" He's more confused, dear, than violent," Mrs. Smee explained. " He seems to think we're doing *The Tempest;* Romeo's tanned breast he takes for Ferdinand's. ' Mind, Ferdy boy,' I heard him say, ' and keep the ——— out.' Whereupon, his mind wandered to the Russian plays I love, and he ran through some of Irina's lines from *The Three Sisters.* ' My soul,' you know she says, ' my soul is like an expensive piano which is locked and the key lost.' Ah, there's for you; Shakespeare never wrote that. He couldn't. Even by making piano, spinet. O Russia! Russia! land of Tchekhov, land of Andrief, of Solugub, of Korelenko, of Artzibashef—Maria Capulet salutes thee! And then my man was moved to sing. His love, she was in Otaheite . . . But as soon as he saw me he was back at *The Tempest* again, calling me Caliban, Countess, and I don't know what."

" Oh, how disgraceful!"

" After the performance I'll pop home—Home!— in a drosky and shut him out."

" Meanwhile? "

" He'll pass for a Friar. The Moujik! "

" Still . . ."

" He'll probably be priceless; the masses always love the man who can make them laugh."

Miss Sinquier moved restlessly towards the door and looked out.

All was activity.

Plants for the balcony set, of a rambling, twining nature, together with a quantity of small wicker cages labelled " Atmospherics," and containing bats, owls, lizards, etc., were in course of being prepared.

The manageress knit her brows.

" Miss Marquis," she called, " instead of teasing the animals, I suggest you complete your toilet."

" . . . She'd better look sharp! "

Mrs. Smee consulted her notes.

" She reminds me more of a nurse-maid than a nurse," she murmured. " Not what *I* should have chosen for Juliet at all."

" Perhaps not."

" Miss Marquis has no stage presence. And such a poor physique—she's too mean."

" Anyway, Sally's got fine men. I never saw finer fellows. Even the Apothecary! Fancy taking the fatal dose from a lad like that; he makes me want to live."

Mrs. Smee purred.

" To have interesting workmates is everything," she said. " Hughie Huntress, as Producer, seemed quite stunned at the subtle material at his disposal. . . . In fact, he realised from the first, he told me, he *couldn't* ' produce ' all of it."

Mrs. Sixsmith lowered her voice.

" Where did Sally find her Balthasar?" she asked, " and where did she secure her Tybalt? "

" My dear Mrs. Sixsmith, I'm not in the management's secrets, remember, so much as you! "

" Or who put her in the way of Sampson and Gregory? And *where* did she get her Benvolio? "

" Through an agent, I don't doubt."

Mrs. Sixsmith threw a sidelong probing glance in the direction of the door. Already in her heart she felt herself losing her hold. Had the time inevitably come to make out the score?

Through the open door came a squeal.

" Sally, the owls! "

" Leave them, Réné," Miss Sinquier ordered.

" *Dearest*, what diddlies; one has a look of old Sir Oliver! " Miss Mant declared, coming forward into the room.

Clad in a pair of striped " culottes," she had assumed,

notwithstanding sororal remonstrance, the conspicuous livery of Paris.

" I just looked in to thank you, darling," she began, " for all your sweetness and goodness . . . Oh, Sally, when I saw the playbill with my name on it (right in among the gentlemen!) I thought I should have died. Who could have guessed ever it would be a breeches part?"

" Turn round."

" Such jealous murmurings already as there are; a-citizen-of-Verona, an envious super without a line, whispered, as I went by, that my legs in these tissue tights had a look of forced asparagus."

" Nonsense."

" Of course: I knew that, Sally. But devil take me. How I'll hate going back into virginals again; these trousers spoil you for skirts."

" Sprite."

" And I'd a trifling triumph too, darling, which I chose to ignore: just as I was leaving my dressing-room, Jack Whorwood, all dressed up for Tybalt, accosted me with a fatuous, easy smile. ' I want your picture, Miss Iris, with your name on it,' he said. ' Do you?' I said. ' I do,' he said. ' Then I fear you'll have to,' I said. Oh, he was cross! But all the while, Sally, he was speaking I could feel the wolf . . ."

" Better be careful," Mrs. Sixsmith snapped.

" As if I'd cater to his blue besoins!"

" Réné, Réné?"

" Although I snubbed him," Miss Iris murmured, stooping to examine upon the toilet-table a beribboned aeroplane filled with sweets, " he looked too charming!"

Mrs. Smee chafed gently her hands.

" I must return to my Friar," she said.

" He is saying the grossest, the wickedest things!"

" Mr. Smee's sallies at times are not for young ears,"

Mrs. Smee loftily observed. " His witticisms," she added, " aren't for everyone."

" My friend, Miss Tird, who came to watch me dress, was quite upset by his cochonneries! "

" Although your little friend appears scarcely to be nine, she seems *dazed* by her sex and power," Mrs. Smee unfavourably commented.

" I'll have to go, I suppose," Miss Sinquier sighed, " and see how matters stand."

" Prenez garde: for when making up he mostly makes a palette of his hand," Mrs. Sixsmith said. " I happen to know—because one day he caught hold of me."

Mrs. Smee protruded her tongue and drew it slowly in.

" Hist! " she exclaimed.

Along the corridor the call-boy was going his rounds.

" First act beginners," chirped he.

Miss Sinquier quivered.

" . . . Soften all hostile hearts and let them love me . . ." she prayed.

XVI

THE sound of rain-drops falling vigorously upon the glass roof awoke her. A few wind-tossed, fan-shaped leaves tinged with hectic autumnal colours spotted marvellously the skylight without, half-screening the pale and monotonous sky beyond.

With a yawn she sat up amid her pillows, cushioning her chin on her knees.

After last night's proceedings the room was a bower of gardenia, heliotrope, and tuberose, whose allied odours during slumber had bewildered just a little her head.

Flinging back the bed-clothes, she discovered as she did so a note.

" Sally," she read, " should you be conscious before I return, I'm only gone to market, cordially yours R. Iris. Such mixed verdicts! I've arranged the early papers on your dressing-table. I could find no reference to me. This morning there were rat-marks again, and part of a mangled bat."

" Oh, those ' atmospherics' ! " Miss Sinquier complained, finding somnolently her way into the inner room.

Here all was Italy—even the gauze-winged aeroplane filled with sweets had an air of a silver water-fly from some serene trans-Alpine garden.

Dropping to a fine *cassone* she perused with contracted brows a small sheaf of notices, the gist of which bore faint pencilled lines below.

" Her acting is a revelation."

" We found her very refreshing."

" There has been nothing like it for years."

" Go to the Source."

" An unfeminine Juliet."

" A decadent Juliet."

" . . . The Romeo kiss—you take your broadest fan."

" The kiss in Romeo takes only fifteen minutes . . . ' Some ' kiss! "

" The Romeo kiss will be the talk of the town."

" A distinctive revival."

" I sat at the back of the pit-stalls and trembled."

" Kiss—— "

" The last word in kisses."

" Tio, Tio, Io! Io! jug—jug! "

" Shakespeare as a Cloak."

" A smart Juliet."

" An immoral Juliet."

" Before a house packed to suffocation——"

" Among those present at the Source last night were"—she looked—" were, Queen Henriette Marie, Duchess of Norwich, Dismalia Duchess of Meath-and-Mann, Lady Di Flattery, Lord and Lady New-blood, Mr. and Lady Caroline Crofts, Sir Gottlieb and Lady Gretel Teuton-Haven, ex-King Bomba, ex-King Kacatogan, ex-Queen of Snowland, ex-Prince Marphise, Hon. Mrs. Mordecai, Lady Wimbush, Lord and Lady Drumliemore, Sir John and Lady Journeyman, Lord and Lady Lonely, Lady Harrier, Feodorowna Lady Meadowbank, Lady Lucy Lacy, Duchess of Netherland and Lady Diana Haviours, Miss Azra, Miss Christine Cross, Sir Francis and Lady Four, Madame Kotzebue, Comtesse Yvonde de Tot, Mlle. de Tot, Duque de Quaranta, Marquesa Pitti-Riffa and Sir Siegfried Seitz."

So . . . she sneezed, all was well!

A success: undoubtedly.

" O God! How quite . . . *delicious!* " she murmured, snatching up a cinquecento cope transformed to be a dressing-gown, and faring forth for an airing upon the stage.

At that hour there wasn't a soul.

The darkened auditorium looked wan and eerie, the boxes caves.

The churchyard scene with its unassuming crosses, accentuating the regal sepulchre of the Capulets (and there for that), showed grimly.

" Wisht! " she exclaimed, as a lizard ran over her foot.

Frisking along the footlights, it disappeared down a dark trap-hole.

Had Réné been setting more traps? Upon a mysterious mound by a jam jar full of flowers was a hunk of cheese.

She stood a moment fascinated.

Then bracing herself, head level, hands on hips, she executed a few athletic figures to shake off sleep.

Suddenly there was a cry, a cry that was heard outside the theatre walls, blending half-harmoniously with the London streets.

XVII

THE rich trot of funeral horses died imperceptibly away.

Looking out somewhat furtively from beneath her veil, Mrs. Sixsmith could observe only a few farmers conversing together beneath the immemorial yews of S. Irene.

It was over.

There was nothing left to do but to throw a last glance at the wreaths.

"From the artists and staff of the Source Theatre as a trifling proof of their esteem "—such the large lyre crushing her own "Resurgam." And there also was the Marys' with their motto: "All men and women are merely players. They have their exits and their entrances." And the "Heureuse!" tribute by the sexton's tools—she craned—was Yvonde de Yalta's, it appeared.

"Yvonde de Yalta!"

Mrs. Sixsmith gulped.

"You grieve?"

Canon Sinquier stood beside her.

"I——" she stammered.

"So many tributes," he said.

"Indeed, sir, the flowers are extremely handsome."

"So many crowns and crosses, harps and garlands."

"One has to die for friends to rally!"

"Were you in her company?"

"I, Canon? . . . I never was on the stage in my life!"

"No?"

" My husband never would listen to it: he holds with Newman."

" . . . I don't recollect."

" Besides, I'm no use at acting at all."

" You knew my poor daughter well? "

" I was her protégée . . . that is . . . it was *I* who tried to protect her," Mrs. Sixsmith replied.

" My dear madam."

" Oh, Canon, why was her tomb not in Westminster where so many of her profession are? I was reading somewhere only the other day there are more *actresses* buried there than kings! "

" It may be so."

" Here . . . she is so isolated . . . so lost. Sally loved town."

" Tell me," he begged, " something of her end."

" Indeed, sir——"

" You're too weary? "

" Oh, I *hate* a funeral, Canon! Listening to their Jeremiads."

" You shall take my arm."

" Her father was her cult, Canon. . . . In that she resembled much the irresistible Venetian—*Catarina Dolfin-Tron.*"

" Sally seldom wrote."

" Her time, you should remember, was hardly her own."

" Tell me something," he insisted, " of her broken brilliance."

" Only by keening her could I hope to do that."

" One would need to be a Bion. Or a Moschus . . ."

" We laid her, star-like, in the dress-circle—out on Juliet's bier . . . Mr. and Mrs. Smee and her dresser watched . . . Berinthia . . . Sylvester . . . came. I cannot lose from mind how one of the scene-shifters said to me, ' How bonny she looked on the bloody balcony.' "

" My poor darling."

" On the evening of her dissolution, I regret to say, there was a most unseemly fracas in the foyer—some crazy wretch demanding back her money, having booked her place in advance; every one of the staff in tears and too unstrung to heed her. Had it been a box, Canon; or even a stall! But she only paid four shillings."

" Was there anything on my poor child's mind distressing her at all? "

" Not that I'm aware of."

" No little affair . . . ? "

" No . . ."

" Nothing? "

" Your girl was never loose, Canon. She was straight. Sally was straight . . . at least," Mrs. Sixsmith added (with a slight shrug) . . . " to the best of my knowledge, she was! "

" In a life of opportunity . . ."

" Ah, sh——, sir, sh——! "

" Had my daughter debts? "

" Indeed she had . . . she owed me money. Much money. But I won't refer to that . . . Sally owed me one thousand pounds."

" She owed you a thousand pounds? "

" She was infinitely involved."

" Upon what could she spend so much? "

" Her clothes," Mrs. Sixsmith replied with a nervous titter, " for one thing, were exquisite. All from the atelier of the divine Katinka King . . ."

" King? "

" She *knew*! Puss! The white mantilla for the balcony scene alone cost her close on three hundred pounds."

" And where, may I ask, is it now? "

" It disappeared," Mrs. Sixsmith answered, a quick red shooting over her face, " in the general confusion. I hear," she murmured with a little laugh, " they even filched the till! "

" What of the little *ingénue* she took to live with her? "

" May Mant? Her sister is sending her to school—
if (that is) she can get her to go! "

" It was her inadvertence, I take it, that caused my
daughter's death."

" Indeed, sir, yes. But for her—she had been setting
traps! She and a girl called Tird! a charming couple!"

" Oh? "

" Your daughter and she used frequently to take
their meals in the boxes, which made, of course, for
mice. There was a well, you know, below the stage."

" So she wrote her mother."

Mrs. Sixsmith fumbled in the depths of a beaded
pouch.

" There was a letter found in one of her jacket-
pockets, Canon," she said. " Perhaps you might care
to have it."

" A letter? From whom? "

" A young coster of Covent Garden, who saw your
daughter at a stage-farewell."

" Be so good, dear lady, as to inform me of its
contents."

" It's quite illiterate," Mrs. Sixsmith murmured,
putting back her veil and glancing humorously
towards the grave.

" DEAR MISS,

" I seed you at the Fisher Mat. on Friday last and
you took my heart a treat. I'm only a young Gallery
boy—wot's in the flower trade. But I knows wot I
knows—And you're It. Oh Miss! I does want to see
you act in Juliet in your own butey-ful ouse, if only
you ad a seat as you could spare just for me and a pal
o' mine as is alright. I send you some red cars sweet
and scenty fresh from Covent Market, your true-gone
                                                    " BILL.

" Hoping for tickets."

" Poor lad. Sally would have obliged him, I feel
sure," Canon Sinquier said.

" Alas, what ephemeral creatures, Canon, we are!"

" We are in His hands."

" She knew that. Sally's faith never forsook her . . .
Oh, Canon, some day perhaps I may come to you to
direct me. I'm so soul-sick."

" Is there no one in London to advise you? "

" Nobody at all."

" Indeed? You astonish me."

" I'm perfectly tired of London, Canon! "

" Your husband, no doubt, has his occupation
there."

" My husband and I are estranged . . ."

" You've no child? "

" Alas, Canon! I often think . . . sometimes . . .
I would like to adopt one. A little country buttercup!
Really . . . a dog, even the best of mannered—isn't
very *comme il faut*."

" You seek a boy? "

" Mer-cy *no!* Nothing of the sort . . . You quite
mistake my meaning."

" Your meaning, madam, was obscure."

" I imply a girl . . . a blonde! And she'd share with
me, sir, every facility, every advantage. Her education
should be my care."

" What is your age? "

" From thirteen——"

" An orphan? "

" Preferably."

" I will discuss the affair presently with my wife,"
Canon Sinquier said, turning in meditation his steps
towards the wicket-gate.

" Before leaving your charming city, Canon, I
should like beyond everything to visit the episcopal
Palace: Sally used often to speak of the art-treasures
there."

" Art-treasures? "

" Old pictures! "

" Are you an amateur of old pictures? "

" Indeed I am. My husband once—Paul—he paid a perfect fortune for a Dutch painting; and will you believe me, Canon! It was only of the back view of a horse."

" A Cuyp? "

" A Circus—with straw-knots in its tail. It used to hang in Mr. Sixsmith's study; and there it always was! Frankly," she added, brushing a black kid glove to her face, " I used sometimes to wish it would kick."

" If you're remaining here any length of time, there are some portraits at the Deanery that are considered to be of interest, I believe."

" Portraits! "

" Old ecclesiastical ones."

" Oh, Canon? "

" Perhaps you would come quietly to dinner. At which of our inns are you? "

" I'm at the ' Antelope.' "

" I know that my girl would have wished our house to be open to you. You were her friend. Her champion. . . ."

" Dear Canon—don't . . . don't: you mustn't! She's at peace. Nothing can fret her. Nothing shall fret her . . . ever now. And, you know, as a manageress, she was liable to vast vexations."

" My poor pet."

" She's *hors de combat*: free from a calculating and dishonest world; ah, Canon! "

" We shall expect you, then, dear Sally's friend, to dinner this evening at eight," Canon Sinquier murmured as he walked away.

Mrs. Sixsmith put up a large chiffon sunshade and hovered staccato before the dwindling spires and ogee dome of S. Irene.

It was one of the finest days imaginable. The sun shone triumphantly in the midst of a cloudless sky.

She would loiter awhile among the bougainvillæas and dark, spreading laurels of the Cathedral green, trespassing obtusely now and then into quiet gardens, through tall wrought-iron gates.

New visions and possibilities rare rose in her mind.

With Sally still, she could do a lot. Through her she would be received with honours into the courtly circles of the Close.

Those fine palatial houses, she reflected, must be full of wealth . . . old Caroline plate and gorgeous green Limoges: Sally indeed had proved it! The day she had opened her heart in the Café Royal she had spoken of a massive tureen *too heavy even to hold.*

Mrs. Sixsmith's eyes grew big.

Her lost friend's father wished for anecdotes, anecdotes of her " broken brilliance"; he should have them. She saw herself indulging him with " Salliana," wrapped in a white mantilla of old Mechlin lace.

An invitation from Cañon and Mrs. Sinquier should be adroitly played for to-night: " And once in the house! . . ." she schemed, starting, as a peacock, symbol of S. Irene, stretched from a bougainvillæa-shrouded wall its sapphire neck at her as if to peck.

Her thoughts raced on.

On a near hill beyond the river reach the sombre little church of S. Ann changed to a thing of fancy against a yellowing sky.

From all sides, seldom in unison, pealed forth bells. In fine religious gaiety struck S. Mary, contrasting clearly with the bumble-dumble of S. Mark. S. Elizabeth and S. Sebastian in Flower Street seemed in high dispute, while across the sunset water S. Ann-on-the-Hill did nothing but complain. Near by S. Nicaise, half-paralysed and impotent, scarcely shook. Then triumphant, in a hurricane of sound, S. Irene hushed the lot.

Mrs. Sixsmith fetched a long, calm breath.

It was already the hour he had said.

" And my experience tells me," she murmured, as she took her way towards the Deanery, " that with opportunity and time he may hope to succeed to Sir Oliver."